"This is the first time I've read
but it definitely won't be the last. She writes from a view
that has you inside her stories, living the lives and
feeling the emotions."

~Happily Ever After Reviews (5 Teacups)

~~*~~

A MAN LIKE THAT

"I finished this in one night, because I had to know
what was going to happen. I even cried a few times
along the way as I felt for the characters with what they
were going through."

~One Hundred Romances Project (5 Stars)

~~*~~

UNWRITTEN RULES

"Ms. Henderson builds up dramatic suspense along
with mountains of romantic insecurity! ...This page-
turner is a true delight. A spicy and fun 'who done it',
which includes a beautiful love story."

~In'D Tale Magazine (5 Stars)

Also by Alison Henderson

Harvest of Dreams
A Man Like That
The Treasure of Como Bluff
Unwritten Rules

Happy Holidays!

Alison

Small Town Christmas Tales

Alison Henderson

Small Town Christmas Tales

ISBN-13: 978-1517253721
ISBN-10: 1517253721

Cover art by Creative Author Services

Published by Alison Henderson
United States of America
September 2015

Dedication

To my writer sisters at The Roses of Prose group blog. Your annual holiday short stories inspired me to go a step further.

If Wishes Were Fishes

She had just one wish for the holidays. The same wish she'd wished every December for the past five years.

Please bring Ben home for the holidays.

What was it Grandma Berta used to say? If wishes were fishes, the sea would be full. When Marlee was a little girl she'd wondered what that meant. Now she thought she understood, but she still couldn't give up hoping.

She tucked an errant red-gold curl behind her ear and leaned forward to peer out the multi-paned bay window at the front of her yarn shop A Stitch in Time. It was only four o'clock in the afternoon, but heavy gray clouds hung low over the small harbor of Porter's Landing, Massachusetts. It would be dark soon, and she could almost taste the coming snow. It looked like they were due for the first white Christmas in several years. She shivered beneath her thick fisherman's knit sweater and hugged her arms around her middle. Snow wouldn't be so bad if Ben were here. As a kid she'd tagged after him and her older brother Matt when they went sledding down Murphy's Hill or built a fort in Barnum's Wood. Any adventure was better with Ben along.

They had grown up as tightly connected as three links in a chain. She'd barely noticed her feelings for Ben changing until suddenly she was a sophomore in high school and the boys were seniors. By then every girl in the school was hot for Ben Granger, and Marlee Farrow was no exception.

But so much had changed since high school. The links had shattered. She hadn't seen Ben in more than five years, not since the awful day of Matt's funeral. Five days after they buried her brother, Ben had left town without a word and joined the Navy. He hadn't been back since.

Her eyes stung, and she squeezed them tight to forestall the flow of tears. *Stop it. You should be stronger by now.*

But even after all this time, the pain was still raw.

Marlee swallowed the lump forming in her throat. Then she sniffed and pulled a tissue from the pocket of her jeans to dab her nose. If only… But recriminations served no purpose. All young men believed in their own invincibility, and Matt and Ben had been no different.

"Marlee, can you take a look at this and see if you can find the mistake? I don't know what I've done." With a half-frown of good-natured confusion, Evelyn Barlow held up a small, misshapen red stocking. Despite her lack of experience and skill, Evelyn was one of the most enthusiastic members of the Knit Wits, a knitting club that met at A Stitch in Time every Thursday afternoon.

Marlee took the sock and quickly spotted the error. "It looks like you dropped a couple of stitches, but I think I can fix them." She deftly recaptured the errant loops on the small metal needle then handed it back to Evelyn.

"Thanks so much, dear. I don't know what I'd do without you."

"Never get that darned ornament finished, that's for sure."

It was hard to be certain who had muttered the comment, but Marlee suspected Helen Carmichael. The Knit Wits were a pretty congenial group, but as the oldest member, Helen felt she'd earned the right to speak her mind, and in true New England fashion, she did so without reservation.

"How are we coming along, ladies?" Marlee glanced at the members seated in a circle on plain wooden chairs, surrounded by cubbies filled with colorful yarns of every description. As the only knitting shop within twenty miles, A Stitch in Time was popular with both tourists and locals, so she tried to maintain a broad inventory.

"I'm done," Helen replied, holding up a cheerful gingerbread man. Her gnarled fingers were still so quick she'd already added the face and buttons.

"Almost there," added Mary Duckworth. "I just need to crochet the hanger for my snowman."

On cue the seven remaining Knit Wits displayed their nearly-complete creations as well. This year the club had voted to donate ornaments for the Christmas tree at the hospital. After the holiday they would be free to any patient who wanted to take one home.

"Then it looks like we're ready for refreshments," Marlee said. "Who wants eggnog?" Hands flew up.

"I'm supposed to be watching my cholesterol," Helen groused.

"I can always fix you a cup of tea."

"Hold on." Helen's eighty-two-year-old eyes twinkled. "I didn't say I didn't want eggnog. I said I wasn't supposed to have it. You won't tell Dr. Grimes, will you?"

Marlee laughed and crossed her heart. "It'll be our secret."

Forty-five minutes later the finished ornaments were packed in a box and the Knit Wits were gathering their coats and knitting baskets. "See you all at the party at the hospital tomorrow," Evelyn called over her shoulder on her way out.

Marlee followed the chattering gaggle and locked the door. As she crossed the uneven old brick street and headed for home, a familiar hollow feeling swelled in her chest. The ache had been building for days despite her best efforts to banish it. She loved A Stitch in Time and the Knit Wits, but she wanted more. Most of her high school friends had traded the quiet of Porter's Landing for the excitement of the city years ago. A few came home for Christmas but it wasn't the same. She missed her family. And although she might not admit it out loud, she missed Ben.

Her parents had moved to Boston after Matt's death, too grieved by the never-ending reminders of their loss, but Marlee couldn't leave Porter's Landing. It was home and where she needed to be. After Grandma Berta died, she had moved from the big square captain's house with its widow's walk on the roof that had sheltered her family for two centuries into her grandmother's tiny shingled cottage covered with climbing roses.

She snuggled deeper into her raspberry mohair muffler and pulled her hat lower as she made her way down the street that ran parallel to the rocky shore. It wasn't snowing yet, but the wind had picked up, tossing whitecaps on the water. Her cottage was only a couple of blocks away, a cozy refuge from the worsening weather, but for some reason she wasn't ready to go home yet. Her restless feet carried her toward the lighthouse on the point.

Since the early nineteenth century, Porter's Landing had been tied to the sea. It had begun as a whaling village then later switched to cod, and a small fleet of fishing boats still left the harbor most mornings in search of the daily catch. Generations of Farrow women had waited, sometimes in vain, for their men to come home from the sea, and Marlee was no different.

Ever since Ben had left, she'd come to the old red and white striped lighthouse whenever the loneliness closed in, to stare out to sea and think of him, wondering where he was and how he was doing. The building itself was locked and no longer in use, but the ground-level observation deck was still open. When she reached it she leaned forward, resting her arms against the metal railing. The clouds overhead had morphed into an angry gray mass.

She repeated her plea like a mantra, as if that might increase its chances of reaching the right ears. *Please bring Ben home for the holidays.*

The summer after graduating from college, he and Matt had come home for a couple of weeks of fun and relaxation before launching into the world of grown-up responsibility. Her heart twisted when she remembered them together: tall, strong, tanned, and laughing. They'd taken her father's small sailboat out past the shelter of the harbor into open water when the skies darkened and a sudden squall blew in. Even though a fishing trawler was within hailing distance, the high winds and waves had swamped the small vessel before help could arrive.

The fishermen managed to pull Ben out, but Matt was lost. She would never forget the agonizing hours before the Coast Guard found his body the next day.

Marlee pounded her fist against the railing. How could Ben have left town without speaking to her? Didn't he understand how much she needed him, how much she needed someone to share the pain? Healing was so hard when you had to do it alone.

She dropped her forehead against her hands and allowed the tears to fall.

"Marlee?" A deep voice interrupted her misery.

She lifted her head a couple of inches. She must be hallucinating.

"Marlee, it's me."

Slowly, she straightened and turned.

"Ben?"

****

He took in her watery blue eyes and the pert little nose that was nearly the color of her scarf. Either his memory was rusty or Marlee Farrow had changed— big time. She was far more beautiful than he remembered. Her eyes narrowed, either in anger or suspicion, and he realized she was waiting for him to respond. "Yeah, it's me."

Her expression remained guarded. "What are you doing here?"

He deserved her cold reception and then some. He just had to get through this and say what he needed to say. Then he could finally close this chapter of his life and move on. "I thought I might find you here. I tried your house, but no one was home. Then I remembered you used to like to come to the lighthouse."

She shifted her gaze to the wind-whipped waves. "It soothes me."

Ben rammed his hands deeper into the pockets of his pea coat. "Even in this weather?"

"Yes."

She wasn't making this easy, but she had no reason to. He forged ahead. "I need to talk to you."

She still refused to look at him. "Go ahead. I'm listening."

He needed to sit down with her, to look her in the eye. "Can't we go somewhere, I don't know…warmer? There must be a coffee shop in town."

She pushed back the sleeve of her coat and glanced at her watch. "The Java Joint will be closed by now. It's two days before Christmas, you know."

He knew all too well. "There must be somewhere else."

Marlee hesitated and he could almost see the wheels turning. "I guess we could go to my house. I moved to Grandma Berta's old cottage a few years ago." She stepped back from the railing and headed toward the path to the harbor.

Ben caught up in two long strides. "My mom told me."

She shot him a quick glance, and his gut clenched at the flash of pain in those lovely blue eyes.

"Funny. She never told me a thing about you." Marlee squared her shoulders and marched ahead.

An ache grew in the pit of his stomach as he stared at her straight back and swinging stride. *Because I asked her not to. I wanted to disappear from your life. You deserved to forget me.*

Neither spoke on the short walk to her house. Ben waited on the tiny porch as she fumbled for her key then opened the crimson door. "Come in," she said. She unwound her scarf and hung it on a peg by the door, along with her hat and coat.

He stepped into the compact living room and waited. He felt as out of place as Gulliver in Lilliput. If he reached up, he could probably touch the ceiling without extending his arm. The cottage was one of a long row that had been built for nineteenth century sailors' widows...or in this case, maybe a hobbit. Marlee, however, seemed perfectly at home in the diminutive space. She headed toward the kitchen, which was little more than an alcove off the main room, filled an old copper kettle at the deep farmhouse sink, and put it on the small gas stove to heat.

"Is tea all right?" she asked.

"Anything hot sounds great."

"You might as well sit down." She gestured toward the round table draped with a vintage flowered cloth that must have belonged to Berta.

He pulled out one of the sturdy ladder-back chairs and sat, trying to remember the words he'd crafted and rehearsed over the past few weeks.

She pushed a bright red pottery mug with hand-painted holly wreaths toward him and took the seat across the table. "All right. You're here. You said we needed to talk, so talk."

Ben wrapped his hands around the mug and stared at the rising tendrils of steam. He'd thought of this moment for months, but now that he was with her, his mind went blank.

"Ben."

Her voice was softer, less angry now. When he raised his gaze, he saw pain in her eyes, but also a hint of longing.

8

She nodded. "I agree. We do need to talk. Since you don't seem to want to start, I will. I've missed you."

Guilt turned the knife. "I've missed you, too, Marlee."

"We used to be so close—you, and me, and Matt."

He stared down at his hands. "I know. But after what happened, I couldn't face anyone, especially you."

"It was an accident, Ben. No one blamed you."

He glanced up. "They should have. I blamed myself. I still do. I should have done more. I was weak and I panicked." Anger and regret churned in his stomach.

Marlee tilted her head. "Could you have saved him?"

He'd asked himself that question a thousand times. "I don't know, but I should have tried harder." He slammed his fist to the table hard enough to rattle the mugs. "Matt was my best friend, like a brother to me, and I let him die."

"The Coast Guard said the storm was too strong. There was nothing you could have done. In fact, you're lucky you didn't drown, too."

"For a long time I wished I had."

"And that's why you ran away and joined the Navy?"

He shrugged. "I had to get away. I didn't care what happened to me. I thought it would be fitting if the sea took me, too."

She took a long sip of the cinnamon-scented tea then sat back in her chair. "You haven't been home in five years. Why are you here? Why now?"

"I had to see you, to tell you to your face how sorry I am about Matt's death." His voice dropped. "I owe you that much."

"I always knew you were sorry."

"I needed to say it."

She reached across the table and gave his hand a quick squeeze. "And I needed to hear it. So what's next?"

He tried to read her emotions in her expression, but her features gave nothing away. "My tour is up, and I've left the Navy."

"Have you come home to Porter's Landing for good?"

"I don't think so." He shifted in his chair and glanced out the window. A few flakes drifted past the pane, highlighted by the streetlight on the corner. "I don't know."

"What are you going to do now?"

"A buddy offered me a job as a mechanic in his garage in Newport News, Virginia. I might take him up on that."

"Is that what you did in the Navy? As I recall, you were a bio major in college."

He shook his head. "I was a medical corpsman, working mostly in physical therapy."

"That sounds rewarding."

His mind flashed to some of the desperately injured, but determined, young men and women he'd worked with. "It was."

Marlee finished her tea, set her mug firmly on the table, and met his gaze head on. "I have an invitation and proposition for you."

Ben's heart skipped a beat. "What's that?"

"Meet me at the hospital Christmas party tomorrow afternoon at three o'clock."

"I don't—"

She held up her hand. "No excuses. Most of the village will be there, including your mom. She comes every year. I'm sure she'd love to have an escort."

He thought of his mother and all the Christmases he'd missed. As long as he was making amends, she deserved more from him, too. "Okay. I'll be there."

****

Marlee closed the door behind Ben and rested her forehead on the back of her hand. *You did it. You saw Ben Granger again and you didn't cry.* Two fat tears rolled down her cheeks.

Over the years, she'd thought up dozens of things she wanted to say to him, from angry accusations to pleas for attention, but when she finally got the chance, she'd said none of them. Those things had been all about her, about her feelings, her loss. As soon as she saw the pain and self-blame clouding Ben's dark eyes, her concern for her own feelings had melted away. She'd spent five years brooding over personal hurts without truly considering what Matt's death must have meant to Ben. Maybe it was a Christmas miracle, but seeing him again had loosened the chains binding her to the past. Now, she needed to find a way to return the gift.

A Stitch in Time was closed the next day for Christmas Eve, so Marlee spent the morning baking a double batch of Grandma Berta's famous German Chocolate Cookies for the party that afternoon. She sifted and stirred, chopped and baked until the heavenly aroma filled the house. When the kitchen became too warm, she opened a window to share the scent with passersby on the sidewalk.

11

A little before three o'clock she stacked the cookies and loaded them, along with the box of knitted ornaments, into her car and drove up the hill to the hospital. When she turned into the parking lot, Evelyn Barlow and Mary Duckworth pulled in behind her in Evelyn's trusty old Toyota. They popped out, and Mary took the box of ornaments while Evelyn balanced two big plastic containers.

"What did you make this year?" Evelyn asked Marlee as they picked their way across the thin layer of snow covering the parking lot.

"The usual—Grandma Berta's German Chocolate Cookies. What about you?"

"I experimented—anise flavored Snickerdoodles. It's no good to let yourself get in a rut, you know."

Marlee grimaced. Evelyn was no better at baking than she was at knitting. *Anise flavored Snickerdoodles?* However, she had to admire the woman's attitude. Evelyn charged through life, cheerfully seeking new challenges. Some succeeded and some didn't, but she seemed to take every experience in stride.

Like most of the town, the dark brick hospital was well over a hundred years old. It had been remodeled inside to keep up with the demands of modern medicine but still retained a few charming features of the original building, such as the large parlor where the annual holiday party was held. Marlee followed Evelyn and Mary through the heavy wooden double doors, where they met several other Knit Wits already at work making punch and arranging the cookie table. A few patients had gathered, and others were making their way down the corridor, helped by nurses.

The party had started years ago as a way to lift the spirits of children who were forced to spend the holidays in the hospital, but soon older patients joined in decorating the tree and singing carols to the accompaniment of the tinny old piano in the parlor. Eventually, it became a tradition for the whole town. For one night the doctors even relented and allowed cookies for everyone who was able to eat them.

While she unpacked her cookies onto the big silver trays, Marlee glanced around to see if Ben and his mother had arrived. He'd better show up as promised, or she would drive to his house and drag him out. But first she had to find Dr. Wiley. An idea had been burrowing in her brain since the previous afternoon.

Thirty minutes later the party was in full swing. The ornaments hung from the tree, music filled the air, and half the cookies had disappeared. She'd managed to corner Dr. Wiley for a short chat, and now all she needed was Ben. Where was he?

A finger tapped her shoulder from behind and she jumped.

She spun around to find Ben and his mother. Angela Granger offered a tentative smile, while her son's expression remained sober.

"It's nice to see you, Marlee."

"You, too, Mrs. Granger." Marlee squeezed her hand. She hadn't seen Angela in several months, but she didn't remember the deep creases marking Ben's mother's skin or the hollows beneath her eyes and cheekbones. Ben's absence had taken a toll on her, too.

Ben touched her shoulder. "I told you I'd come."

She raised her gaze to his, searching for a clue to his thoughts. "Yes, you did. Thank you." When his eyes remained a dark mystery, she turned to his mother. "Why don't you get some punch and a cookie, Mrs. Granger? I know Evelyn would love to show you the

13

ornament she knitted this year. I'd like to borrow Ben for a minute."

Angela smiled and patted Ben's arm. "I'll see you later, sweetie."

Marlee watched her make her way through the crowd to join Evelyn and several other Knit Wits at the punch bowl. "You mom's glad to have you home."

I'm glad to have you home.

Ben frowned. "I should have come sooner."

"Maybe you weren't ready."

His frown eased, and a smile teased his lips as he met her gaze. "How did you get to be so wise? You were just a kid the last time I saw you."

"It's been a long time. I'm not a kid anymore."

"No, you're not."

The warm undertone in his voice kindled a corresponding heat in her middle. She reached for his arm. "I have a surprise for you."

Ben raised his brows but allowed her to half-drag him across the room to where Dr. Wiley sat talking with a young man in a wheelchair.

"Dr. Wiley, this is Ben Granger."

The older man stood and shook Ben's hand. "Glad to meet you. Marlee tells me you were a corpsman in the Navy."

Ben shot her a skeptical glance before replying. "Yes, sir. I've just finished my tour."

"She also tells me you worked in PT."

Ben nodded.

"Any experience with spinal cord injuries?"

"Yes, sir. Between combat injuries and accidents, I've pretty much seen it all."

"Good. There's someone I'd like you to meet." Dr. Wiley stepped back and gestured to the young man beside him. "This is Mark. He's just about the age you were when you left Porter's Landing. About a month ago he was hit by a drunk driver and lost the use of his legs. We hope it's temporary, but only time and hard work will tell."

Ben smiled at Mark. "It isn't easy and it isn't fun, but don't give up. I've seen amazing things happen."

"You know, you might be able to help Mark with his recovery. We're short-staffed in PT and could really use an experienced therapist. Would you be interested?"

Ben slowly turned to Marlee. "Was this your idea?"

Heat rose in her cheeks, and she lifted her chin a fraction. "You said you weren't sure about your plans. I wanted to make sure you had plenty of options."

"You don't have to decide right away," Dr. Wiley added.

"Thanks, I'd like to think it over for a couple of days."

The doctor clapped him on the shoulder. "No problem. The new year's a good time to start a new life."

"Yes, sir." He turned. "Marlee, could I speak to you someplace a little quieter?"

Uh, oh.

She summoned a brilliant smile. "Of course."

Ben took her hand in a firm grip and led her to a spot near the doorway, away from the crush of partygoers.

Every nerve in her body jangled. "Now before you say anything—"

He slid one arm around her, pulling her close, and raised a finger to her lips. "Ssh."

She stilled and scanned his face. He looked different, lighter, as if a crushing weight had been lifted from his shoulders. His eyes held a new spark.

"I want to thank you," he said.

"You're welcome, I guess."

He leaned forward and pressed a soft kiss to her forehead. "Thank you for being you, for interfering, for caring about me." He kissed the tip of her nose.

"I've always cared about you."

"I care about you, too." He pulled her closer and tilted his head to glance up at the sprig of mistletoe dangling from the arched opening above them. "The doctor was right. The new year is a good time to start a new life."

Then he bent his head and met her lips in a kiss filled with all the promise and hope the holidays could offer.

Mistletoe and Misdemeanors

This was the last place she expected to spend Christmas. Callie Rayburn glanced around the puke-green cinder block cell in the basement of the Hawthorne Springs, Missouri police station. In jail for Christmas. It figured, given the downward spiral her life had taken during the past twenty-four hours.

A tear slid down the side of her nose. She dashed it away with the back of her hand and snuffled. She didn't even have a tissue because that jerk Billy Freeman had taken her purse. What kind of town let a pubescent little snot like Billy Freeman wear a badge and carry a gun? It seemed like just last week she'd babysat him and his obnoxious younger brother to earn enough money to buy her dream dress for the senior prom.

Another tear followed the track of the first. If Billy Freeman was old enough to be a police officer, what did that make her? Ancient. Over the hill. Thirty years old with nothing to show for it. Two days ago she'd been living the high life in St. Louis with a job, a cute apartment she couldn't afford, and a future. Today—zip, nada, bupkis. And now, to tie the whole thing up with a big fluffy bow, she'd been arrested by Billy Freeman for breaking and entering. Un-freaking-believable.

Disgusted, she pulled out of her slouch and straightened her spine. If Officer Billy thought she was going to take this lying down, he had a lot to learn. She might have temporarily sunk to the level of pathetic loser, but heaven help her, she would sleep in her car before she spent Christmas Eve in a jail cell.

Callie shot another glance around her barren surroundings. Where was a tin cup when you needed one? Wasn't that what prisoners used in the old movies? She'd have to settle for her shoe. She was lucky this pair didn't have laces—Billy probably would have taken them to keep her from hanging herself.

She slipped off one sleek black ankle boot and thumped it against the metal bars, wincing at the resulting scuff that marred the smooth surface. Damn. She loved those boots. She hadn't even paid the credit card charge for them yet.

"Billy Freeman, you little weasel, let me out of here!" she shouted at the top of her lungs.

Nothing.

"Billy, if you don't unlock this door right now, I'm going to tell your mother!"

Still no answer.

Her righteous indignation slipped a notch. Surely he hadn't locked her up and abandoned her to spend the whole miserable holiday alone. She was starving. Even the condemned got a last meal, didn't they?

"Billeeeeeeee!"

The big metal door from the stairwell clanged open, and a man stepped through. But it wasn't Billy Freeman. This man was taller, broader, and darker. His brows drew together in a fierce scowl.

"Stop that caterwauling. I sent Officer Freeman home to spend Christmas Eve with his family."

Double damn. It was the man himself, Chief Thomas H. Blackstone, AKA Tommy Blackstone, the hottest, baddest boy in Hawthorne Springs High School. A devil in worn denim. The kind of boy girls yearned to regret. Callie and her older sister had been no exception.

During the fall of her freshman year she had watched Susan sneak out their bedroom window every Saturday night for six weeks to ride off into the dark on the back of Tommy Blackstone's magic motorcycle. Her jealous, fourteen-year-old imagination had concocted a whole array of shocking and titillating scenarios, which Susan refused to confirm or deny. Each time, her sister had slipped back through the window an hour before dawn with a dreamy smile on her face and a finger pressed to her lips.

The infatuation had burned itself out quickly, and since Susan hadn't nursed a grudge or broken heart, Callie had never squealed to their parents. Over the past fifteen years Tommy Blackstone had drifted off her radar screen. At some point Susan had mentioned he'd joined the Marines after graduation then returned to Hawthorne Springs and become a police officer. But by that time Callie was in St. Louis, clawing her way up the ladder in the marketing department at Van Pelt and Van Pelt Advertising. She'd never crossed paths with Tommy on her brief visits home. Then again, she'd never managed to get arrested before, either.

She gritted her teeth in a facsimile of a smile. "Since *Officer* Freeman is gone, you can let me out. I'm sure you've got the key there on your super-duper police utility belt."

He nodded. "I do, but you're not going anywhere."

"Tommy Blackstone, you let me out of here!"

He turned his attention to the clipboard in his hand. "My friends call me Tom. You can call me Chief Blackstone, but I still can't let you out. You were caught breaking into an unoccupied residence—"

She threw her hands in the air and rolled her eyes. "My parents' house! I lost my key."

His stern expression didn't falter. "Tell it to the judge. You also resisted arrest. You bit Officer Freeman—I saw the teeth marks. I ought to charge you with assaulting an officer."

"He put his hand across my mouth!"

"To shut you up. You were creating a disturbance."

Callie gave an unladylike snort. "I remember when you used to create plenty of disturbances. When did you become such a hard-ass?"

"You don't want to know."

His tone stopped her cold, and a flippant response died on her lips. She regarded him critically for the first time. He still bore a passing resemblance to the rebellious hell-raiser she'd secretly pined for in high school, but he'd changed. He stood taller and straighter now. His lean jawline could have been carved from granite, and his dark blue eyes held a new gravity. Devil-may-care Tommy Blackstone might have left Hawthorne Springs, but tough, serious Tom had returned in his place.

He flipped the papers on his clipboard back into place. "Besides, based on your behavior, I'm not convinced you're not a danger to yourself or others."

"Don't be ridiculous. I've never been a danger to anyone."

His fine, firm lips tilted up in a slow smile. "I don't know about that."

****

Callie Rayburn was cute when she scowled. Heck, she was cute anytime with her soft, shoulder-length brown curls and snapping green eyes. She'd grown up to be quite a looker. He could barely see a hint of Susie's gangly, gawky fourteen-year-old sister in the furious woman before him.

Tom glanced at his watch. He was due at his mom's house for supper after she got off work. He hadn't expected to be stuck at the station. Why did Callie Rayburn have to go and get herself arrested on Christmas Eve?

Grabbing the back of a heavy oak chair, he dragged it across the speckled green linoleum floor to the cell and sat facing her with his forearms resting on his knees. "Let's start at the beginning."

She crossed her arms. "Let's start by you letting me out of this cell."

"Sorry, can't do that."

With a huff of frustration, she sank down on the gray metal cot and sent him an imploring look. "Can't you let me out on bail or something?"

"I don't set bail. That's Judge Cameron's bailiwick, and he's playing the lead wise man in the Christmas pageant at Springside Baptist Church this evening. I'm not about to risk divine retribution by interrupting the performance."

She lifted her chin. "I'm sure my parents will be home soon, and we can clear this whole thing up."

He sat back and regarded her. "You don't know, do you?"

"Know what?"

"Your parents left yesterday afternoon for a Christmas cruise to Mexico with your sister and her family."

Her mouth sagged open, and her shoulders slumped as the fight drained from her body. Tears welled in her lovely green eyes, drowning the fire that had burned a moment earlier. "H-how could they?" She blinked, and a tear rolled down each cheek.

Her pain hit him like a fist to the solar plexus. It had been much easier to see her locked in a jail cell when she'd been all prickly and defiant. Now he felt like he'd kicked a kitten. He softened his voice. "Callie, why are you here? Your mom said you weren't coming home this year, that you couldn't get away from work."

"I wasn't going to." Her voice caught and she cleared her throat.

"So what happened?"

She turned away and dabbed her tears with the back of her hand. "My plans changed."

"In what way?"

"It's none of your business." She sniffed loudly. "You need to keep tissues in these cells."

"Callie, look at me and tell me what happened. Maybe I can help."

She spun around, eyes blazing again through her tears. "I got fired, all right? There's not much you can do about that."

Fired? The last he'd heard, her career in St. Louis was on the fast track. According to her mom, Callie was slated to become the youngest vice president in the history of her firm. When she snuffled again, he grabbed a box of tissues off a nearby desk and poked them through the bars.

She blew her nose then wiped it. "Thanks."

22

"Why don't you tell me about it?"

"It was last night, at the office Christmas party."

"You got fired at a Christmas party?" It took a pretty cold-hearted bastard to fire someone at a Christmas party.

She blew her nose again and glared at him. "Do you want to hear this or not?"

"Sorry, go on."

She hiccupped and blotted the corners of her eyes. "By the time the party started, Mr. Van Pelt Junior had already warmed up pretty well with the bottle of vodka he keeps in his lower left desk drawer. After a rousing speech about what a good year we'd had, he called us into his office one by one to hand out the Christmas bonuses."

"And you didn't get a bonus?"

A bitter laugh broke from her lips. "Oh, he had a special bonus in mind for me. The problem was, I wasn't interested."

Slow-burning rage consumed the remnants of his guilt. "Did he put his hands on you?"

"He tried."

His hands balled into fists. *The bastard.* He flexed his fingers to relax his fists then drew a deep breath. "And...?"

She glanced down at the floor, apparently fascinated by the random black dots on the linoleum tiles. "I discouraged him."

"The whole story, Callie."

Her chin came up and her rueful gaze caught his. "All right. I may have discouraged him with a brass lamp...to the head."

"He deserved that and worse."

"I'm not sure the police would have seen it that way. Junior told me to get out or he'd call the cops. At the time, I considered myself lucky not to be arrested." She gave him a tight half-smile. "Little did I know that pleasure was yet to come."

"It really hasn't been your day, has it?"

"Oh, it gets worse."

Assaulted, fired, and arrested – all in less than twenty-four hours. How much worse could it get?

"I was shaking so hard I barely made it back to my apartment, and when I got there I found an eviction notice taped to my door. Apparently the owner sold the building, and the new owner plans to turn it into condos."

"You could buy one of the condos."

She looked at him as if he'd grown a second head. "With what? I just lost my job. I couldn't even afford the rent."

"What are you going to do?"

She shrugged. "Beats me. I loaded everything I could fit into a U-Haul this morning and drove here, hoping to find comfort in the bosom of my family. Do you have any idea how hard it is to find a U-Haul on Christmas Eve?"

Tom pushed to his feet and reached for his keys, his decision made. "I don't think it will jeopardize the safety of the good citizens of Hawthorne Springs if I let you out until you can appear before Judge Cameron on the twenty-sixth."

She popped up. "I'm glad you finally see reason."

"Don't get so excited. I'm going out on a limb and remanding you to my own custody."

Her brows drew together, and her eyes narrowed. "What exactly does that mean?"

24

He sighed and thrust the key into the lock. "It means I'm taking you with me."

****

A tiny thrill rippled through Callie's chest. Tommy Blackstone was taking her home with him! Too bad Susan was out of town. A sudden childish urge to stick her tongue out at her sister popped into her head before she quashed it. How ridiculous. She and Susan were grown women. Susan was happily married and had two children, for Pete's sake.

Tom held the door and she stepped out of the cell. "Where's my purse?"

He opened a battered brown file cabinet, removed her bag, and handed it to her.

"I'll need some fresh clothes and my toiletries, too." She glanced down at her rumpled green sweater and grimaced. "I might have gotten a little sweaty loading the U-Haul. All I could think about was getting away from St. Louis as fast as possible and coming home."

"Your car and the trailer are in the lot out back. You can pick up some things on the way."

On the way to where? Unease slithered into her mind. Wild Man Tommy Blackstone might have morphed into Respectable Hard-ass Chief Tom Blackstone, but in truth she barely knew him. What had she gotten herself into?

As if he could read her thoughts, his dark blue eyes crinkled at the corners, and a smile teased his lips. "I'm taking you to my mom's house."

Callie remembered Helen Blackstone as a harried single mother who'd struggled to raise her son on the income from her small beauty shop after her husband abandoned them. They used to live in a rundown trailer park on the edge of town.

"I moved her into a nice little house on Myrtle Street when I left the Marines."

Triple damn. On top of everything else, the man had become a world-class mind reader.

Their footsteps echoed through the empty police station as Tom ushered her to his cruiser parked out back next to her sporty blue hatchback. She bit the inside of her cheek. She loved her car, but without a job, it was another luxury she could no longer afford.

He opened the cruiser door. "Get in and give me your keys. I'll put your suitcase in the trunk."

She complied and in a couple of minutes they were on their way to Myrtle Street. Tom pulled to a stop in front of a modest white ranch house with a string of twinkling lights outlining the porch and a festive holly wreath on the door. After retrieving her suitcase, he led the way up the walk and opened the door. A comforting, spicy aroma embraced her as she stepped into the front hall.

"Mom, I've brought you an unexpected holiday guest," he called.

Helen Blackstone walked through the arched opening to the dining room, wiping her hands on a dishtowel. When she saw Callie, her lined face brightened. "Callie Rayburn, what a surprise!"

Nerves fluttered in Callie's stomach. Despite the fact that everyone in Hawthorne Springs knew everyone else, at least by sight, she and Tom's mother were virtual strangers. "Hi, Mrs. Blackstone."

Tom set her suitcase on the braided rug and unzipped his jacket. "Callie's folks are out of town, and she lost her key."

She held her breath. *If he mentions the arrest, I'll die right here.* He turned his head away from his mom and gave her a slow wink that sent her pulse skipping.

Helen smiled. "Then you must stay here, dear. Tom, take her bag to the guest room. The chili's ready, so we'll eat as soon as you both wash up." She turned and headed in the direction of the kitchen.

Callie followed Tom down the hall to a small, neat room with blue-and white striped wallpaper and an old cherry wood bedroom set. "I can't stay here," she whispered.

He raised one dark brow. "You'd rather spend the holiday in jail?"

"Your mother doesn't even know me."

His teasing smile did nothing to calm her jitters. "Then you're in luck—she doesn't know what a pain in the butt you can be. And if you manage to behave yourself for a couple of days, she might never find out."

"Dinner's on the table!" Helen's muffled voice called from the dining room.

After Tom ladled the steaming chili into bright blue bowls, Helen passed a basket of soda crackers. "I hope this isn't too spicy for you. Chili is a Christmas Eve tradition at our house."

Callie smiled and gave her bowl an appreciative sniff. "I love chili and it smells great."

Helen reached for a bowl of shredded cheese. "How long will you be in town, dear?"

Good question. "Um, my plans are kind of up in the air at the moment."

"You mustn't think I'm trying to get rid of you. You're welcome to stay as long as you like. I just figured you'd have to get back to work. Your mom will be so

27

disappointed she missed you. She talks about you every time she comes in to get her hair done."

Callie's stomach sank. She'd been too upset about losing her job to consider her parents' reaction to the disintegration of her career.

"Callie's looking for a new employment opportunity, Mom." Tom sent her another wink, causing her to fidget in her chair. That must be how he'd charmed the pants off half the girls in high school. The man was a menace.

Helen's spoon clattered in her bowl. "Here in Hawthorne Springs? Oh, that's wonderful! Your mother will be thrilled!"

She hesitated before responding. "Um, I'm not so sure."

Helen reached for Callie's hand and gave it a squeeze. "Trust me, she'll run through the streets shouting the news. She's proud of your success in the city, but she's said many times how much she misses you and wishes she could see more of you."

If only Tom's mother was right.

Helen monopolized the rest of the dinner conversation, offering ideas about local businesses that could use help with marketing. By the time Callie and Tom finished drying the dishes, her tired brain was dizzy with possibilities. A huge yawn slipped out before she could stifle it.

Tom glanced at his watch. "I should go. Walk me to the door."

He stopped just inside the foyer and turned. "So, are you going to stay?" His voice dropped to a husky near-whisper that sent jolts of energy zinging through her.

Whoa. She took a half-step back. How had Susan spent six weeks in this man's company without

28

spontaneously incinerating? Of course, he'd been much younger then. Maybe he hadn't developed his full powers yet.

She swallowed hard and assumed what she hoped was a nonchalant expression. "I don't know what I'm going to do. I'd thought I would come home until I got my bearings. I hadn't considered staying in Hawthorne Springs for good."

A single masculine dimple appeared in his cheek. "Well, think about it." He leaned down and planted a swift kiss on her cheek. "See you tomorrow." Then he was out the door.

She stood riveted to the floor with her hand frozen on the knob as he backed his cruiser down the driveway. *What just happened here? Did Tommy Blackstone kiss me? Me?*

****

The next morning, Callie awoke fuzzy-headed. She'd had a weird, yet oddly satisfying, dream about locking Billy Freeman and Junior Van Pelt in the House of Horrors at the Hawthorne Springs summer carnival. Then Tom Blackstone had arrived with the keys. Killjoy. Yet she'd been happy to see him. Why?

She opened one eye a crack to see unfamiliar striped walls. *Where am I?* Deciding she was too tired to care, she drifted back to sleep until the aroma of bacon and hot cinnamon rolls pierced the fog.

A knock sounded on the door, and Helen Blackstone stuck her head in. "Merry Christmas, dear. Are you awake? Tom has arrived, and breakfast is ready."

Callie shoved her mass of tangled curls aside. *Tom? Here? Now?* "Have I got time to shower?"

Helen shook her head. "Not unless you like cold bacon. I brought you a robe in case you don't have one." She stepped into the room and held out a quilted pink garment that looked like it might have belonged to Tom's grandma.

"Thank you, but I've got clothes in my suitcase. Just let me wash my face and run a brush through my hair. I won't be a minute."

Helen smiled. "You'd better hurry. We don't want to keep Santa waiting."

Santa?

Callie grabbed clean underwear, a pair of jeans, and a red cable-knit sweater from her bag then raced to the bathroom. Three minutes later she slid into the kitchen, slightly out of breath. Tom sat at the table wearing a brown plaid flannel shirt and munching a thick slice of crispy bacon.

"Merry Christmas." He eyed her from the head to toe. "Nice socks."

Callie glanced down at her fuzzy scarlet socks with the dancing polar bears. She loved fun socks, and this was one of her favorite pairs. If Big Chief Tom couldn't appreciate the wonderfulness of them, he needed a serious attitude adjustment.

Helen bustled in with a steaming coffee pot. "Have a seat, dear. We never open presents until after breakfast."

Presents. The word conjured a sudden memory of long-ago Christmas mornings when she and Susan used to race downstairs in their matching flannel nightgowns to discover the bounty Santa had left under the tree while they slept. Why had her family picked this, of all years, to take a cruise? A tiny pang of abandonment poked her in the chest.

Then she scolded herself; she was thirty, not thirteen. She might not have her family, but at least she wasn't alone for Christmas. She just wished she had a present for Tom's mother. She made a mental note to buy Helen something nice as soon as possible to thank her for being so kind and opening her home to a stray for the holiday.

After finishing the biggest, richest, most sinful cinnamon roll she had ever eaten, Callie was ready to call it a day and head back to bed when Helen announced it was time for Santa to do his duty. Stifling a yawn, she followed her hostess into the small living room where Tom stood next to the tree, wearing a crimson Santa hat. An unexpected laugh escaped her lips at the sight of the stern Chief Blackstone looking so ridiculously festive.

Tom gave her a mock frown, but his indigo eyes twinkled with humor. "No laughing. Presents are serious business."

Callie replied with a snappy salute. "Yes, sir."

He proceeded to check the tags on the packages under the tree, handing one to his mother then taking one for himself. Callie watched while they opened their gifts and admired the scarf Helen had knitted for Tom and the bottle of perfume he'd purchased for her. They continued taking turns until only a single gift bag remained.

At least Callie assumed it was a Christmas gift. Pictures of pumpkins, skeletons, and black cats adorned the garish orange bag. She was even more stunned when Tom picked it up and handed it to her with a flourish. "This is for you."

She accepted it gingerly. What kind of weird joke was this?

Tom's lips thinned. "The convenience store at the gas station on Route 43 was the only place open at ten o'clock last night, and that's the only bag Charlie could find in the storeroom. Just open it."

Helen chose that moment to excuse herself and made a strategic exit to the kitchen with the dirty dishes.

Callie reached into the tissue paper in the bag and pulled out a DVD of a twenty-year-old romantic comedy that had always been one of her favorites. She held it up with a delighted smile. "Thank you! How did you know?"

The tense lines around Tom's mouth relaxed. "I have my sources." He motioned to the bag. "Keep going—there's more."

She reached into the bag again and pulled out another DVD of a similar vintage sci-fi movie about giant subterranean worms attacking a small Nevada town. She raised her brows in questioning disbelief. "Really?"

This time Tom grinned. "Hey, it's a cult classic. Trust me, you'll love it. The worms look fantastic on my sixty-two inch screen."

A sudden suspicion popped into her head. "These wouldn't happen to be from your personal collection, would they?"

He shrugged. "I didn't have a lot of options. Charlie's Truck Stop doesn't carry a wide inventory. Of course, if you'd rather have a bag of stale pork rinds—"

She clutched the DVDs to her chest as if they were priceless treasures. "Oh, no! They're perfect—just what I always wanted."

"I'm glad to hear it."

"But I do have a question. Did you intend for us to watch these together?"

His lips curved in a lazy smile. "I'll watch yours if you watch mine."

Yikes! Stay cool. Keep it light. If the atmosphere in Helen's living room got any hotter, clothes were going to have to come off. Callie forced a playful smile. "How could I resist an offer like that?"

"You can't." He pushed to his feet with an annoyingly satisfied look on his face. "I've got to go to the office for a few hours. I'm splitting the shift with Officer Freeman so he can spend Christmas morning with his kids."

Her brows popped up in surprise. *His kids? Billy Freeman is a father? I really must be a hundred years old.*

"I'll be back in time for dinner," Tom continued. "Afterwards, we can go to my place for movie night."

She swallowed hard. *Ready or not, here I come.* "That sounds great."

He reached for her hand and pulled her from the sofa. "Walk me to the door." When they reached the front hall, he still held her hand. "Yesterday you said you didn't know. I'm hoping for a more definitive answer today."

Her mind went blank. *What was the question?*

"Have you decided whether or not to stay in Hawthorne Springs?"

Oh, that. A lot had happened since yesterday, but she didn't have an answer, at least not yet. She pressed her lips together and contemplated a particularly fascinating pink flower on the wallpaper behind his left shoulder. "I'm still thinking about it."

He took her other hand and tugged until she stepped closer. His arms slid around her. "Maybe I can help you make up your mind." With a slow, sexy smile, he lowered his head until their lips met.

When he drew back, she smiled. "I have to admit the idea is growing on me."

Let it Snow

She'd never seen a Santa suit used in quite that way. Jillian Mayberry leaned forward against the steering wheel of her Mini Cooper and squinted through the swirling snow. Her eyes weren't playing tricks on her. That really was a bright red Santa suit flapping in the wind from the flagpole in front of the old log cabin. A lighted sign above the door spelled out *Santa's Workshop* in hand-carved red letters. Thank heaven, she'd found it. She wasn't sure she could drive another mile in this storm.

That morning she'd left St. Paul under a cold, bright sun, but by the time she'd reached Duluth a light snow had started to fall. Now, a few miles up the north shore of Lake Superior past Two Harbors, it looked like two armies of snow giants were having a pillow fight—and the pillows were losing. The fat flakes were so close together she could barely see the log building ahead. She inched forward a few feet and stopped her car next to a big brown SUV with a Minnesota Department of Natural Resources insignia on the door.

She flipped up the hood of her long down coat and reached for the briefcase on the seat beside her. Leave it to Alan, Jr. to dump this chore on her before hopping a jet for a skiing holiday in Aspen with his new girlfriend, one of the many perks of being the son of the founder of the most prestigious private family office firm in St. Paul, which catered to the legal and financial needs of some of the wealthiest families in the state. As the most junior member of the firm—and Alan, Jr.'s *former* girlfriend— Jillian was low woman on the totem pole, so this last minute task had naturally fallen to her two days before Christmas.

Oh, well. It didn't really matter since she wasn't going home for the holidays anyway. She'd been feeling sorry for herself ever since her mother had announced her plans to spend Christmas in St. Tropez with her latest flame, Ricardo. Jillian huffed out a sigh, and a cloud of vapor fogged the windshield. She should be impervious to being hurt by her mother after all these years, but somehow she wasn't.

She glanced at the log cabin again through the thickening snow. At least this was a simple assignment. She just had to get a couple of papers signed. With any luck she would be in, out, and on her way within a few minutes—which was a good thing. The highway was already heavily snow-packed, and she worried about making it back to the shelter of the motel room she'd booked in Two Harbors.

When she stepped out of the car, a gust of wind snatched the door from her hand and slammed it shut. She was so startled she lost her footing and sat down hard in a knee-high pile of snow. Muttering under her breath, she struggled to her feet. Whatever had possessed her to leave Virginia for this god-forsaken icebox? Oh, yes. The lure of a well-paying job at

Saperman, Ellis, and Saperman, along with those pesky student loans.

Her socialite mother had considered law school a waste of time and money, so Jillian had cobbled together the funds to pay her own way. At the moment, with her nose running and fingers and toes numb, she wondered whether she should have caved and gone the debutante route. Remembering the requisite small talk with silly, overdressed people at endless rounds of parties, she decided freezing to death was preferable. It hadn't been easy, but she'd scrimped and saved every penny during the past five years to pay off the last of her loans. Only one more payment and she could tell Saperman, Ellis, and Saperman—specifically Alan, Jr.—what they could do with their job.

And go where? Do what?

With no ready answer, she picked up her fallen briefcase, sighed, and trudged through growing drifts to the door.

Up close, the cabin appeared to be at least eighty years old with dark hand-hewn beams and wide white chinking. Warm light beckoned from a pair of curtained windows flanking the rustic paneled door. Jillian raised a gloved hand to the big knocker carved in the shape of a grinning Santa and brought it down with a resounding thud. Teeth chattering, she counted the seconds until the door swung open and Paul Bunyan peered down at her. Okay, so maybe he was Paul Bunyan's beardless, blond, cuter brother, and wearing a dark green ranger's uniform with a patch on the shoulder that read Gooseberry Falls State Park instead of plaid flannel and denim, but he was mighty impressive all the same.

His brows drew together in a formidable frown. "What kind of fool goes shopping in weather like this?

37

You'd better come in." The giant grabbed her arm and pulled her through the door into a warm, gingerbread-scented Christmas wonderland.

The cabin might have started life as a humble pioneer homestead, but now it housed a mind-boggling array of Yuletide décor—a veritable explosion of red and white. Jillian blinked twice, trying to take it all in. Against one wall a fire crackled in a fireplace of smooth, round river rocks. Shelves lined the other walls, and a couple of tables and chairs peeked through the holiday mayhem. Every inch was filled with carved wooden Santas, red and white painted bird ornaments, and ribbon-wrapped animals and wreaths fashioned from straw. In the middle of it all stood a floor-to-ceiling Christmas tree, twinkling with tiny white lights and covered with wooden ornaments in the shapes of animals, toys, and elves in tall, pointed, red hats.

"Wow." The word slipped out under her breath. She'd never seen anything like Santa's Workshop in her life. Her minimalist, modern art-loving mother would have fainted if confronted by such colorful confusion. To Jillian, the place was magic.

"It's something, all right. My grandpa made most of them."

She'd almost forgotten the giant. She had also almost forgotten her mission. She flipped back her hood and pulled off her gloves, stuffing them in the pockets of her coat. Pasting a smile on her face, she stuck out her hand. "I'm not a customer. I'm Jillian Mayberry, from Saperman, Ellis, and Saperman."

His big, warm hand engulfed hers, even as his brows drew together in a confused frown. "Erik Gustafsson."

Gustafsson. Good. He was the man she'd come to see. He also had eyes the color of a fjord in summer.

Where on earth did that come from?

She'd never been prone to poetic flights of fancy. She gave her head a tiny shake to rid it of such nonsense.

But he's so tall, and strong, and blond. Like a Viking warrior, but with better hair and minus all the scars.

Stop that, you moron! You've got a job to do — do it.

With reluctance, she withdrew her hand and nodded. "Mr. Gustafsson, I've brought you some papers on behalf of our client, Ronald Oglethorpe."

Suspicion entered Erik's gaze. "What kind of papers.

Jillian fumbled in her briefcase, pulled out a folder, and handed it to him.

He read the first page, and a muscle in his jaw flexed. He turned to her with a scowl. "This is an eviction notice."

"Let me see that." Jillian snatched the papers from his hand. Lawyers didn't serve eviction notices. They left that unpleasant duty to the sheriff's office. Surely Alan, Jr. hadn't sent her on such a fool's errand. She could kick herself for not reading the contents of the folder before she left. She'd been annoyed and in a hurry to beat the storm, but neither was an acceptable excuse for allowing herself to be caught unprepared.

She scanned the first page. "It's not an eviction notice. Technically, it's a notice exercising the termination provision in your lease."

Erik crossed his arms across the breadth of his chest. "I don't think so."

She sighed and silently cursed Alan, Jr. "There's no need to make this more difficult than necessary. It's a straightforward legal document. If you'll sign next to the arrows, I can be on my way."

His expression remained implacable. "You've got the wrong man."

"You are Mr. Gustafsson, aren't you?"

"Yes."

"And you currently rent this property?"

"No."

She knit her brows, echoing his frown. "I don't understand."

"I told you, you've got the wrong man."

Frustration found a chink in her professional armor. "I need to speak to the lessee of this property, whoever he is." The termination might be an unpleasant legal action, but it was legal. If this man thought he could make it disappear by intimidating her, he was mistaken.

Erik stared at her for a long moment, as if weighing his options. Then he turned his head and called over his shoulder, "*Farfar*, you have a visitor!"

Jillian leaned to peer around him. When a figure emerged from the back room, her mouth fell open, and the folder slipped from her fingers, sending papers wafting to the floor.

Holy, moly. It was Santa Claus. That rat, Alan, Jr., had sent her to evict Santa Claus two days before Christmas.

"Ms. Mayberry, this is my grandfather, Gustav Gustafsson."

Santa smiled and took her hand. "Please call me Gus."

Except for his customary red suit—which was apparently flapping from the flagpole out front—he looked exactly like the illustrations in her cherished childhood copy of *The Night Before Christmas*. Same rosy cheeks, same bushy white beard, same little round belly—well, maybe not so little.

The surrealism of the moment hit home. She was shaking hands with Santa Claus.

"*Farfar*, Ms. Mayberry is here to kick you out."

Gus gave her a cherubic smile. "I'm sure that's not true."

Jillian swallowed hard. How could she do this? But how could she not? It was her job. She bent down, scooped up the papers from the floor, and stuffed them back in the folder. "I'm afraid the owner of this property has decided to invoke the termination provision of your lease. I need you to sign these papers."

A look of confusion crossed Gus's face. "Even though he passed away last month, I can't believe Sam Oglethorpe would let that happen. We grew up together."

At the waver in his voice, Jillian clenched her teeth. If Santa started to cry, she was going to murder Alan, Jr. the minute he got back in the office.

Erik placed his hand on his grandfather's shoulder and gave it a small squeeze. Gus sniffled and blinked a couple of times before regaining his composure. "I don't understand. Sam always said this place was mine as long as I wanted it."

She frowned and opened the folder to check the documents. "These papers indicate the owner is a Ronald Oglethorpe."

"That's Ronnie, Sam's son. There must be some mistake. I'm sure you'll figure it out." Gus pulled out a big red handkerchief, blew his nose, and gave her a watery smile.

Alan, Jr., you're a dead man walking.

Jillian glanced at her watch. It was after six. No one would be in the office this late on December twenty-third, and Alan, Jr. was still in the air on his way to

Aspen. "I'll do what I can to get more information, but I'm afraid it will have to wait until tomorrow."

Gus's smile blossomed. "I'm a pretty good judge of character, and I have complete faith in you."

She wished she shared his confidence. He seemed like such a sweet man. If there was a way out of this mess for him, she would find it, but even a good lawyer couldn't work miracles.

Gus patted his belly. "Now that we've put that worry behind us, I'm hungry. I've got a pot of potato soup on the stove and homemade gingerbread in the oven. Take off your coat and we'll eat."

For a moment she was tempted. The cabin was warm and cozy, and mouth-watering smells emanated from the kitchen. Besides, who wouldn't want to eat dinner with Santa? But the Mini Cooper wasn't a very big car, and if she stayed much longer, she might end up stranded. She retrieved her gloves from her pockets and started to pull them on. "That's a lovely invitation, but the weather is horrible, and I need to get back to Two Harbors while I still can."

Erik crossed to the front window and flicked back the curtain. Clumps of thick, white flakes tumbled down like puffs of cotton candy. "I wouldn't count on it tonight unless you drove here in a snowplow."

She rushed to the window and shoved the curtain aside. The flagpole had disappeared behind a veil of white. Her nerves tightened. "I can't even see my car."

Gus poked his head around her shoulder. "All the more reason to join us for dinner. If the storm passes by the time we finish, Erik can dig your car out and follow you into town to be sure you make it. If it's still snowing, you can both stay here. There's plenty of room."

Sleep here? With Santa and the Viking? That would make some story for her grandchildren — if she ever had any — but it was completely out of the question. "Oh, no, I couldn't."

Erik stepped back from the window. "Well, you're not going anywhere right now, so you might as well eat."

He was right. She had no other option. The least she could do was be gracious. She tucked her hand through Gus's bent elbow and smiled. "In that case, I'd be delighted."

They walked through a smaller room, also chockfull of Christmas decorations, and into a cheery, old-fashioned kitchen. Gus seated Jillian at a sturdy pine table, then joined her while Erik dished up steaming bowls of dilled potato soup and added wedges of chewy pumpernickel.

As they ate and talked, night settled on the cabin. The soup was fabulous, delicate and hearty at the same time. When her spoon clinked against the bottom of the bowl, Gus laughed and declared her an honorary Swede. To her surprise, Jillian found herself spilling the story of her life, up to and including the humiliation of finding Alan, Jr. in the coatroom of the fanciest restaurant in St. Paul draped all over Brunhilde the Berserker — aka the assistant coach of the U of M women's volleyball team.

When she finished, Gus took her hand. "I hope you gave that fellow the old heave-ho. You're much too good for a knucklehead like that."

She wondered if she could adopt Gus as a grandfather. Her own mother had berated her for letting such a "good catch" slip away.

By the time Erik served the gingerbread with lemon sauce, even he seemed to have decided she was no longer Simon Legree's henchwoman. His blue gaze warmed, and his knee brushed hers under the table more than once. When he rose to clear the table, she jumped up to help.

Hands full, he shook his head. "Go check the weather."

The thought of leaving the cozy cabin to drive to a motel sent a shiver through her, but if the snow had stopped, she had no excuse to stay. When she pulled back the curtain and saw the swirling flakes, her selfish internal voice cheered. "It's still snowing, and the wind's picked up," she called out.

"Give me your keys."

She jumped and spun around at the sound of Erik's deep voice behind her.

A half-smile played around his lips, accentuating the sexy masculine dimple on one side. "I'll get your bag and show you to the spare room."

A few minutes later, Jillian followed Erik as he carried her bag down the hall to the spare bedroom. She was about to spend the night in an isolated cabin with two men she'd just met. Of course, one of them was Santa, so that must make it all right.

He opened the door to a picture out of *Northwoods Home* magazine—a hand-carved log bed with plump pillows and a red and white reindeer comforter, wrought iron light fixtures, and a braided rag rug on the floor. Even the switch plate by the door was carved in the shape of a black bear.

He set her bag on the bed. "The bathroom's through there. I'll be in the room next door if you need anything."

She turned to face him. "Thank you. I'm sure I'll be very comfortable. It was kind of Gus to put me up for the night."

His blue eyes twinkled. "You didn't expect Santa to send a lady out into a storm like that, did you?"

She grinned. "He is the spitting image, isn't he?"

Erik returned her smile. "He tries hard." Then his expression sobered. "He's a great old guy, and he doesn't deserve what your client is trying to do to him."

"No, he doesn't. I promised I'd try to find a way out for him, and I will."

"I hope so. He's counting on you." He stood with his hand on the doorknob. A brief flash of longing crossed his features. "Well, good night."

"Good night," Jillian echoed softly as he closed the door.

While she donned her flannel PJs and brushed her teeth, she tried to recall everything she'd learned in law school about leases. There must be some angle she could use to help Gus. Santa's Workshop was his life, and she didn't want to be a part of taking it from him. She climbed into bed, pulled the covers up to her chin, spread the papers from the folder on her lap, and began to read.

****

The next morning, she woke to the tantalizing aroma of bacon. Her lips curved into a smile before she opened her eyes. When was the last time she'd eaten bacon? Her mother refused to have it in the house, and since she'd started working, Jillian hadn't had time in the morning for more than a quick tub of yogurt. If she wanted to claim a slice before Erik and Gus demolished it, she'd better get moving. Besides, her late-night research had yielded a startling result, and she couldn't wait to share it.

45

Twenty minutes later, showered and dressed, she made her way to the kitchen and found the men half-way through a mountain of scrambled eggs, blueberry pancakes, and crisp bacon.

Erik popped up and pulled out the extra chair. "Have a seat. I made plenty. I'll bring you a cup of coffee."

She smiled at his manners—Alan, Jr. would have left her to fend for herself. "Thanks. Everything smells wonderful."

Gus speared another slice of bacon from the platter. "Erik's a darned good cook."

"Every woman's dream," Jillian quipped. She suppressed a grin at the color rising up Erik's freshly-shaven cheeks.

Gus's eyes twinkled just like Old Saint Nick's. "Yes, he is."

"Eat your breakfast," Erik grumbled.

After several bites, Jillian set her fork down. "I have some wonderful news. I read through the papers last night, including a copy of the original lease, and—"

Gus raised a hand. "Not now."

She frowned. "But—"

The old man patted her hand. "I knew you'd solve the problem, but we can wait until supper to find out how. It's Christmas Eve, you know. Lots to do."

Erik set his napkin aside and rose from the table. "And I've got to start digging us out."

The storm. She'd completely forgotten. "Did it stop snowing?"

"Take a look."

Jillian hopped up and hurried to the front window. She pulled the curtain aside and stared. She'd lived through a few Minnesota winters in the city, but this was different. The scene outside was pure nature, untouched by the hand of man. The snow glittered like slivered crystals as the early morning sun reflected off each individual flake on the ground, the trees, and the mound she assumed was her car.

Erik joined her at the window, peering out over her shoulder. "I haven't heard the plows go by on the highway yet."

She could swear she felt the heat radiating from his flannel-covered chest against her back. "Do you think I'll be able to go home this afternoon?"

"Do you have someplace you need to be for Christmas?"

His warm breath stirred the hairs on top of her head, sending an involuntary shiver down her spine. She pictured the lonely apartment that had never felt like home. "Not really."

His arm slid around her shoulders. "Then why bother? I know Gus would love to have you stay for the holiday."

She turned her head against his shoulder "Will you be here?"

His blue eyes crinkled at the corners. "Umm-hmm. And I bet you've never celebrated a traditional Swedish Christmas Eve. You wouldn't want to miss that." He bent his head slowly toward hers.

"No, I wouldn't." Her lashes drifted down, and her lips parted.

"Then it's all settled!"

Jillian and Erik broke apart at the sound of Gus's voice. His smile was innocent, but the twinkle in his eye suggested he knew exactly what he'd interrupted. "You kids go out and play in the snow. Jillian, you can help Erik uncover your car and clear the driveway."

Three hours later she was exhausted, but had never had so much fun outdoors. She cleared the snow from her car while Erik's oversized snowblower made short work of the driveway. Afterward, they built a magnificent snowman and had an impromptu snowball fight. When they trooped inside, Gus met them with leftover dilled potato soup. After lunch, Erik flopped on the family room sofa to watch football, and Jillian re-read the copy of Gus's original lease. She wanted to be absolutely certain she was right before raising his hopes.

By five o'clock, night had fallen, a fire crackled in the fireplace, and Gus announced it was time for the *Julafton smörgåsbord*. Jillian took her place at the table and stared at the array. Christmas ham, pork sausage, herring salad, pickled herring, home-made liver pâté, rye bread, and potatoes.

Pickled herring? She swallowed hard.

Erik chuckled at her reaction. "Just be glad *Farfar* and I hate *lutfisk*."

She shook her head. "I don't even want to know."

Jillian was still pushing the pickled herring around on her plate when Gus announced, "Now for the best part—the *risgrynsgröt*."

She must have made a face, because Erik leaned over and whispered, "It's rice pudding with raspberry jam."

That sounded better than herring, but she had something she wanted to say first. "Before we get to that, there's something I need to tell you." Gus smiled and nodded, so she continued. "As you know, Ronald Oglethorpe wants to invoke the termination clause in your lease." Gus nodded again. "Well, there was a copy of the original lease included in the folder with the termination paperwork. I read it to the end, including all the addenda, and found a stipulation stating that upon the death of the original owner, Mr. Gustav Gustafsson is to have right of first refusal to the property, and if he chooses to exercise that right, the property is to pass to him free of charge. It seems neither Ronald nor the attorneys at Saperman, Ellis, and Saperman, bothered to read the document all the way through."

Gus beamed and patted her hand. "You've given me the perfect Christmas present, my dear. Now I have one for you. Erik, will you serve the *risgrynsgröt?*"

Jillian had never cared much for pudding — it always reminded her of being in the hospital — but Gus's *risgrynsgröt* wasn't half bad. At least not until she bit down on something hard. She surreptitiously deposited it in her spoon and eyed it with suspicion.

"Ah, you got the almond." Gus clapped his hands together.

At her blank look, Erik gave her a teasing grin. "Tradition says the one who gets the almond will marry during the coming year."

His words brought a sudden pang. "That's unlikely. I'm not even dating anyone."

Gus shook a playful finger at her. "You never know. Don't be so quick to dismiss tradition."

Erik popped another spoonful into his mouth then grimaced and slid a similar nut into his own spoon. He pointed the spoon at Gus. "Tradition says only one almond."

Gus laid a finger aside his nose and winked. "Sometimes tradition needs a little help."

The Brightest Jewel

The ancient Greeks believed amethyst protected against drunkenness. Brianna Cahill wondered if Howard Littleman, Black Bear Creek's perpetually put-upon mayor, knew that when he chose the stone for his wife's Christmas present. Ever since their senior year in high school, Andrea Littleman had been infamous for her ability to drink most males under the table. More likely, Howard was simply trying to extricate himself from yet another domestic pickle. Brianna wondered what it was this time. He forgot to pick up the kids after choir practice? He ran over the trash cans in the driveway? He set the oven to *Clean* instead of *Bake*? Howard was a great guy, but he could be absent minded at times. Brianna couldn't complain, however. The large, flawless amethyst he'd chosen for Andrea was the most expensive stone in her shop.

With a firm grip on the tweezers, she carefully placed the sparkling purple gem into the setting she'd created. A swoop of silver caressed the square cut amethyst, magically holding it secure. One final polish and she could slip it on the chain. She'd promised to have the necklace ready for Howard to pick up first thing in the morning.

The bell above the front door jingled, interrupting her train of thought. Brianna frowned and glanced at her watch. It was late — after seven o'clock. There shouldn't be any customers in The Hidden Gem at this hour. Her assistant Shirley must have forgotten to lock the door when she left at six. She slipped the necklace into her safe, spun the dial, and hurried out to the main shop floor to greet her after-hours visitor.

A tall, dark-haired man in a perfectly tailored cashmere overcoat stood just inside the door, stomping his feet in an attempt to shake the snow off his polished black shoes. He looked more like an investment banker than a smash-and-grab thief, but these days one couldn't be too careful, even in a backwater town like Black Bear Creek, Colorado.

Brianna approached, taking care to stop where she could be seen through the shop's plate glass window, just in case. "I'm sorry, but we're closed for the day."

She sucked in a quick breath when the man met her gaze with eyes the color of her best aquamarine, fringed with thick dark lashes. Then he frowned and spoiled the effect.

"I don't want to buy anything. I'm looking for Dennis Hanover." His words were clipped, his tone brusque.

The fine hairs on the back of her neck stirred. What did this ill-tempered fashion plate want with Denny? Men in Black Bear Creek didn't dress like that. He looked more like an actor in a movie — maybe a gangster movie. A top tier hit man might wear a cashmere overcoat, mightn't he?

"You won't find Denny here."

The man's exasperated expression intensified. "I didn't expect to. I hoped you could point me in the right direction. Your shop seems to be the only place in town that's still open."

"It's not open," she reiterated. When he sighed and ran a hand through his hair, she noticed fine lines and shadows around those aquamarine eyes. Apparently being a hit man was exhausting work.

"No. I guess not." He pulled off a glove and thrust his hand toward her with a tired smile. "Look, I think we got off on the wrong foot. My name is Max Morgan."

She hesitated a second before taking the hand he offered. It was large, warm, and strong. "Brianna Cahill."

Max released her hand. "I'm sorry if I seemed abrupt and I'm sorry to intrude, but I've had a hell of a day. I flew into Denver from New York this morning, and I've been fighting that piece-of-junk rental car for the past eight hours."

She followed his glance through the door to a small beige sedan parked at the curb. "Didn't the agency have anything with four-wheel drive? You won't get far in the mountains in that."

"I figured that out several hours ago. I'm lucky it limped this far, but at least it got me to Black Bear Creek. Do you know where I can find Mr. Hanover? I'd like to see him tonight. If we can come to an agreement quickly, I can be on my way back to Denver in the morning before the next storm hits."

Brianna leaned toward the window and peered out at the closest streetlight. No sign of white flakes. The forecasters were calling for clear skies for the next couple of days, and she hoped they were right. The town's Holiday Jubilee was scheduled for tomorrow evening.

She turned to Max. "I imagine Denny is at Hanover House. Where are you staying?"

"I have a reservation there. I need to check the place out thoroughly. My company is thinking of buying it."

She sucked in a quick breath before releasing it. So much for the hit man theory. Although a savvy assassin might want to diversify his investments, he probably wouldn't buy a hotel in an old mining town high in the Rockies.

She tilted her head and caught her lower lip between her teeth as she pondered the enigma of Max Morgan. Denny had been trying to sell Hanover House for months, ever since she'd turned down his latest marriage proposal. Although she had serious doubts about his current plan to move to Malibu and open a surf shop, she wished him well. Denny was sweet, but over the past ten years his annual proposals had become the stuff of local legend. They would both be happier if he found a way to move on with his life, preferably somewhere away from Black Bear Creek. Max Morgan and his company might offer the perfect solution.

Then she pictured the hotel's leaky roof, peeling trim, and antique plumbing. Her hopes sagged. "I hope your company has deep pockets. Hanover House isn't the showplace it once was. It's going to take quite a bit of money to bring it up to modern standards."

Max smiled. "All the better. My company specializes in buying distressed properties. We plan to tear the old building down and build a modern lodge in its place. Poor condition will only bring the price down."

Tear it down?

Her breath caught in her chest. Hanover House was the heart and soul of the town. It might be shabby, but Brianne had always loved the grand old red-brick Victorian structure that dominated the square. After her father died when she was six, she and Denny had spent every weekday afternoon for several years racing through the wide hallways and stealing cookies from the kitchen under the watchful eye of his grandmother until Brianna's mom came to collect her after work. Hanover House represented familiarity and comfort at a dark and scary time in her life.

And she wasn't the only one. The whole town loved the old place. Denny's ancestors had founded the hotel well over a century ago, when Black Bear Creek was a thriving silver town. His grandmother would never have left the hotel to him if she'd had any idea he might allow it to be torn down. Brianna tried to picture a modern ski lodge in its place, but her mind rebelled. "You can't tear it down!"

****

Max tried to brush aside the unexpected pang of guilt at the lovely brunette's horrified expression. Buying rundown hotels was his business. Usually everyone involved was happy with the bargain. The former owner pocketed a nice chunk of change; the community replaced an eyesore with a clean, modern structure; and Morgan Properties acquired a profitable new asset. Occasionally, some community activist protested the loss of a local "landmark", but over the years Max had become adept at smoothing ruffled feathers.

"You don't need to worry. Our hotels are first class. I have some brochures in the car I can show you."

Brianna shook her head. "I'm sure they are, but that doesn't matter. Hanover House is the heart of Black Bear Creek. It's the oldest building in town and represents our local history. Couldn't you just fix it up?"

He'd heard that question before, too many times to count. "I've seen a lot of old hotels, and in my experience it's more cost-effective to tear them down and build new from the ground up."

Her chin lifted, blue eyes flashing. "What about the history, the charm? Do you figure that into the cost?"

He tried to deflect her anger with a smile. "Our guests seem to find that modern plumbing has its own charm."

Her expression merely hardened. "So change the fixtures. I can recommend a very good plumber."

Brianna Cahill was as stubborn as she was beautiful. Unfortunately, after the day he'd had, Max's patience had worn thin. He tried calm reason once more. "I wish it were that simple. When I inspect the building, I expect to find that all the pipes running through the walls and floors need to be replaced, as well as the electrical and heating systems."

She crossed her arms in front of her chest. "You must run into that all the time in your business. If you're not up to the challenge, maybe you should look for another hotel to buy. We don't need your New York money here."

New York money? He wished. He'd hoped to come home to Colorado with a financing commitment in hand, but no such luck. He and his brother wanted to expand the business, but he'd been unable to convince the bankers he'd met with in New York that Morgan Properties would be an excellent investment for their clients. That meant a tight budget for the next project with no room for failure. He needed to get Hanover House at the right price to be able to swing the deal without outside financing.

He winced as a painful muscle spasm gripped his lower back. *Damn.* Why had he picked this week to get routine maintenance done on his truck? If he'd left it parked at the Denver airport, he could have driven to Black Bear Creek in comfort instead of suffering eight hours of bone-rattling torture in the poorly-sprung sub-compact.

He ran a hand through his hair again and expelled a breath. "Look, Ms. Cahill, we're clearly not going to see eye to eye on this subject tonight. I've had a long day, and I'd appreciate it if you could direct me to Hanover House. After I get some rest, I'll talk to Mr. Hanover and conduct a thorough investigation of the property in the morning before making a decision."

"By all means." She stepped past him, opened the door, and pointed to a hulking structure across the square. "It's right over there."

He narrowed his eyes, trying to pick out the details. With only a couple of windows lit from inside, the old building looked more like a haunted house than a functioning hotel. He'd be doing the town a favor by tearing it down. He stepped out onto the sidewalk. "Thanks. I'll take it from here."

Her smile reminded him of a lioness baring her teeth before she retreated into her shop and closed the door in his face. Max winced again as he folded his length into the mini death trap on wheels. He couldn't understand why Brianna Cahill's antagonism bothered him so much but it did. He'd always prided himself on being able to turn negative situations around. It was an important part of his business. There had to be a way to win her over. The new hotel would be good for Black Bear Creek. He'd even be willing to keep the original name if that would help. He blew on his hands to warm them then shifted into *Drive* and headed toward the hotel.

****

Brianna awoke early with a plan. She'd spent the evening trying to come up with an idea to thwart Max's intention to replace Hanover House with a tacky, modern motel. Ultimately, she had decided the best strategy would be to emphasize the old hotel's defects. It was a long shot, but if poor condition would drive the price down, maybe she could persuade Denny to hold out for a higher offer from another buyer who would be willing to rehab the place. Even though she wouldn't marry him, they'd known each other since kindergarten and were still friends. Maybe he would listen to her.

She took a quick shower, threw on jeans and a sweater, and hurried down the hall to the kitchen. In keeping with the size of her cabin, the kitchen was compact and efficient. Cozy, the realtor had called it. But Brianna loved the warmth of the old knotty pine cabinets, and it was large enough to suit her needs.

She opened the cupboard holding her baking equipment and pulled out a big ceramic bowl and a muffin tin. She'd checked her tiny pantry the night before and had everything she needed. Her scheme involved showing up bright and early at Hanover House bearing breakfast. Business had been so slow lately Denny had been forced to let his cook go, and he was all thumbs in the kitchen. Brianna figured a basket of warm, homemade blueberry muffins with her signature streusel topping should get her through the door. Once inside, she could put her plan into motion.

By six-thirty she had loaded the basket of steaming muffins into her Jeep and was on the road. Twenty minutes later she stood on the steps of Hanover House. Since Denny was currently running the place alone, he kept the heavy oak front door locked from midnight until seven in the morning. She rang the bell and waited. And waited. She rang again. And waited. She was about to go around back to the kitchen door when the old lock clicked and the door opened.

She took a short, involuntary step back. Max Morgan stood in the doorway, looking nothing like the slick banker/hit man who'd showed up at her shop the evening before. His black hair was slightly damp, and instead of an expensive suit, he wore a plaid flannel shirt, jeans, and cowboy boots. His clothes were soft, worn, and fit his lean, hard frame like a custom-made glove. No high ticket, city slicker duds here.

She held out her basket. "I brought breakfast. May I come in?"

He stepped back. "Sure. Denny had to run an errand, so I'm here by myself."

So much the better. Maybe Denny will be gone long enough for me to feed Max and give him the tour from Hell – starting with the basement. Brianna smiled, stepped inside, and offered the basket.

Max flipped back the tea towel covering the muffins and sniffed. "Those smell fantastic."

"I made a dozen."

His aquamarine eyes twinkled. "All for me?"

She shrugged and let her smile take on a flirty edge. "You're the only one here."

"You're here, too, and I insist you join me. I made a fresh pot of coffee."

She hadn't taken time for breakfast before leaving the cabin and had spent nearly half an hour in an enclosed car with a basket of warm blueberry muffins. It didn't take much to convince her. "It's a deal."

He carried the basket and followed her to the old-fashioned kitchen. He set it on the cracked Formica counter while she pulled mugs and plates from the battered cupboards. "You seem to know your way around this kitchen."

"I used to play here as a child." She poured the coffee and set the mugs on the counter.

He snagged a stool and a muffin and dove in. A warm glow kindled in Brianna's midsection at the expression of sheer bliss that crossed his face with the first bite.

"Mmmm, thith ith fantathtic," he murmured with his eyes closed. Then his tongue flicked out to capture a few errant bits of streusel that clung to his lips.

She stifled a grin at the hum of satisfaction buzzing deep inside. Somewhere, maybe buried under her degree in geology, she must have a touch of domestic goddess. There were few things more gratifying than watching a man truly appreciate her cooking.

They sat side by side at the counter, munching and chatting, as the kitchen brightened with the rising sun.

"So how long have you owned your shop?" Max asked as he poured them both a second cup of coffee.

"Two years next month. It's a lot of work but I love it."

"I didn't have a chance to look around much, but from what I could see, you've got some amazing stones. Where do you get them?"

"They're all from Colorado. I dug most of them myself from stream beds and outcroppings around here."

His brows rose. "Wow. I thought you were a jeweler."

Brianna shook her head before taking a long sip from her mug. "The jewelry began as a side line. I've always been a rock hound, but after college I found out quickly there aren't many jobs for geologists unless you want to work for a big oil company."

"Well, your jewelry is beautiful—very original. I thought I might pick up a piece for my mom for Christmas. Would you help me choose something?"

She laughed. "What merchant could turn down an offer like that? The shop opens at ten, but if you're busy you can come by this evening during the Holiday Jubilee. There will be hot cider and caroling in the town square. It's always lots of fun and very festive."

His smile faded. "I'll have to see if I'm still in town."

Her good mood collapsed like a popped bubble. She'd enjoyed her early morning breakfast with Max so much she'd forgotten why he was here—to demolish Hanover House. She needed to stick to her plan to convince him the hotel would be a poor investment and send him on his way as quickly as possible. No sale at The Hidden Gem was worth the loss of Hanover House.

She snatched up the dirty dishes and carried them to the sink. "Since Denny isn't back yet, why don't I give you a tour of the place? I know it almost as well as he does."

He seemed startled. "Um, sure. Okay."

She dried her hands on a tea towel, grabbed a couple of flashlights from the pantry, and faced him with a hard, bright smile. "Great. Let's start in the basement."

****

Max followed Brianna down a rickety flight of steps that must have been as old as the hotel. A dank, musty smell greeted them, and the weak glow from a single, dangling bulb lit their way. When a spider web hit him square across the face, he brushed it away impatiently.

"I'm not sure it's safe to be down here without hardhats," he grumbled.

"Don't say I didn't warn you." She flashed her beam toward an enormous octopus furnace in the corner.

He hadn't seen a gravity furnace like that in years. "Don't tell me that thing is still in use."

"Yep. It's been here since they added central heating in the 'twenties.'"

"At least that explains the temperature in my bathroom this morning."

She led the way to a rusty panel attached to one wall and pried open the lid to display a row of antique glass fuses—not nearly enough for a building this size.

A frown creased his brow. "I'm amazed the place hasn't burned down."

"Now you know why the rooms don't have televisions. Denny's grandma used to say it was for the romantic atmosphere, but it's actually a lack of circuits."

He'd seen enough. "We might as well go back upstairs."

"But you haven't seen the plumbing yet."

"I don't need to. I already knew every system would need to be replaced in order to keep the old place running. But like I told you before, that's not my plan."

She turned back toward the stairs. "At least let me show you some of the other guest rooms. I want to be sure you have the information you need before you make Denny an offer."

The hotel was basically worth the cost of the land with a little extra thrown in for the use of the historic name. What more information did he need?

They reached the top of the stairs and stepped into the kitchen, where Brianna put both flashlights back in the pantry.

"Which room are you staying in?" she asked.

"Number seven, at the top of the stairs and to the right."

She nodded. "Then I bet Denny didn't show you the fourth floor or the attic."

"No, but I really don't think that's necessary. I—"

She grabbed his hand and pulled him toward the lobby and its broad main staircase with elaborately carved newel post and spindles. "I may not be a builder, but even I know you can't judge a building without examining the foundation and the roof. You've seen the basement, so now it's time to see the attic."

Max smothered a grin. Did she hope to discourage him by making him climb a few stairs? If so, she was in for a disappointment. Outside of work, climbing was his passion. Whenever he and his brother could spare a few hours away from the business, they slipped off to go rock climbing in the mountains. After he closed the deal for Hanover House, he'd have to invite her to go for a climb.

He allowed her to drag him along, enjoying the strength of her grip. He admired a woman who wasn't afraid to work with her hands, and as a geologist, Brianna Cahill was clearly as much at home swinging a pickaxe as plying a pair of jeweler's tweezers.

When they reached the fourth floor, the ceilings dropped from twelve feet to eight, and the wood molding around the doors and windows became much simpler. Brianna led him through a warren of utilitarian cubicles with high, tiny windows and peeling paint on the ceilings. "These used to be the servants' quarters."

She seemed to have forgotten she was still holding his hand, and Max wasn't about to remind her. He enjoyed the feel of her too much. "And you brought me up here to see. . .?"

She pointed to a dark brown stain on the ceiling above their heads. "The roof leaks."

"I expected it to."

"I imagine it would be very expensive to replace."

He nodded. "I imagine so." Then he glanced across the hall and noticed another room with a curved front wall. "What's that?"

"Oh, that's one of the turrets."

Turrets? It had been so dark when he arrived last night he hadn't registered the fact that the old building had turrets. He'd loved turrets since he was a kid. "Let's go look." Keeping hold of her hand, he pulled her with him.

The turret room was magical. Each of the six custom-made windows had bowed molding and glass that perfectly matched the curve of the wall and looked out over the snow-covered town square. Across the square the morning sun gilded the majestic, pine-covered slopes of the Rockies.

Max tightened his grip on Brianna's hand. "What a view."

"It is pretty special." Then, as if it had almost slipped her mind, she added, "But don't forget what a money pit this place would be."

63

His mind had already begun to whir with possibilities and plans. "Don't worry. I got the message, loud and clear."

****

Brianna glanced up from the cash register when the bell above the door to The Hidden Gem jingled again. What a day! She'd barely had a chance to catch her breath since opening the shop. Howard Littleman had been waiting when she arrived at ten. He'd declared the amethyst necklace the most beautiful thing he'd ever seen and whipped out his credit card without batting an eye at the price. Now, it was just after seven o'clock, and the Holiday Jubilee had already been a smashing success. So far she'd sold three necklaces, five rings, and a stunning, polished amethyst geode. She handed the gift bag with the geode to the smiling middle-aged woman from Kansas.

The woman grinned. "My brother will love this."

Brianna returned her smile. "I'm sure he will. Thank you so much. Enjoy the rest of your holiday." When the tourist left, she bent down behind the counter to get some more gift boxes.

"How's business?"

Her stomach tightened when she recognized Denny's voice. She'd been on edge ever since she'd left Max at Hanover House that morning. Had her ploy succeeded, or had she merely made him more determined than ever to buy the grand old lady and tear her down?

She straightened and forced a smile. "Business is booming."

Denny grinned. "Great! For me, too."

Max stepped out from behind him with a lidded paper cup in his hand and an unreadable expression on his face. "We brought you some hot cider."

"Thanks." Brianna took the cup, her hand barely registering its warmth.

"I'm moving to California right after New Year's," Denny announced, beaming.

Her heart sank. That could only mean she'd failed. "You sold the hotel."

"I sure did. Got a great price, too."

Damn.

"Signed the papers this afternoon." Denny glanced toward the door. "I want to find Howard Littleman and give him the good news."

The mayor was bound to be thrilled about the new hotel, but Brianna felt like crying. She stared at Denny's back as he scurried out the door.

"You don't have to look like somebody died."

She turned her attention to Max, anger churning inside. "Somebody did. Or at least she will as soon as you move into town with your wrecking ball."

He nodded toward the cup on the counter. "You should drink your cider before it gets cold."

"I do not want any cider," she said between gritted teeth.

The look in his eyes softened, and he reached for her hand. She tried to pull away, but he held tight. "There isn't going to be any wrecking ball."

Brianna frowned. "What?"

"It worked."

"What worked?" He still wasn't making sense.

"You convinced me."

Of what? She tugged on her hand and managed to jerk it free. "I don't understand. Denny said you offered him a good price. Only a fool would pay market price for a building in that condition, especially to tear it down. And no matter what else you might be, you don't strike me as a fool."

Max straightened. "I'm not. I plan to make a handsome profit from my investment in Hanover House—without a wrecking ball."

"Do you expect it to crumble to dust on its own and blow away?"

"Nope. Despite decades of deferred maintenance, the old girl still has strong bones and more than her fair share of charm."

Brianna couldn't believe what she was hearing. "Don't tell me you plan to—"

"Fix her up?" He grinned. "When I'm finished, Hanover House will be the jewel of the Rockies. Black Bear Creek will be a destination, not just a drive-through on the way to the ski slopes."

She groped blindly for the stool she kept behind the counter. "I think I need to sit down."

"It was the turrets that did it, you know."

She nodded numbly. He wasn't going to tear the hotel down. He was going to fix it up.

"When I stood in that turret room, I knew I couldn't duplicate the history and charm in one of our modern lodges."

"But the cost. . ."

Max shrugged. "Will be what it is. I'm a pretty good project manager, and I know how to get things done efficiently. But I won't cut corners on Hanover House. I want to make the most of the existing assets."

"Like what?"

He leaned forward to grab a small gift bag and pencil from behind the cash register and began sketching. "For example, there are four floors with two turret rooms apiece. If we join them with the adjacent smaller rooms like this, we can create spectacular suites that will easily go for four or five hundred dollars a night in season. With antique and reproduction furnishings and fixtures and a little advertising in the right places, I bet we can fill the place year round."

"You're excited about this." Wonder filled her voice.

"I am. So excited I plan to manage this project personally on site."

Brianna struggled to take in the implications of what he was saying. "But what about the rest of your business?"

"My brother can manage it from our office in Boulder."

"Boulder? I thought you were from New York City."

He shook his head. "I'm a Colorado boy, born and bred."

"You plan to move here," she said softly.

A slow smile lifted his lips and lit his aquamarine eyes. He reached for her hand, and this time she didn't pull away. "I'm looking forward to it. This town is full of surprises. Hanover House may be a great business opportunity, but it's far from the only attraction in Black Bear Creek."

Heat rose in Brianna's cheeks, but she couldn't tear her gaze away from the warmth in his eyes.

He leaned toward her across the counter and tugged her hand until she met him halfway, their lips a mere whisper apart. "When I wasn't looking, I found the brightest jewel of all."

Penguins, Pucks, and Pumpkin Pies

A ringing phone at two in the morning never brought good news.

Ellie Markusson's heart pounded as she fumbled for her phone on the bedside table. Was it her mom? Had something happened to Grandma Pearl? She'd seemed fine that morning, but at her age anything could happen.

Her pulse slowed when the caller ID showed Burkhalter instead of Markusson but sped up again almost immediately. Why would her best friend call in the middle of the night? Maybe it was the baby. Clare was eight-and-a-half months pregnant with her second child. Maybe she'd gone into labor and her husband Karl had been called away. That happened to ministers sometimes, didn't it?

"Hello." She was already plotting the fastest route from her friend's house to the hospital in Eau Claire.

"Ellie?" Clare's voice was high-pitched, on the verge of hysteria.

In the background, muffled shouts interspersed with a variety of thuds and bangs. "Clare, are you okay? Where are you?"

"I'm at the food bank. You'd better get down here." Her friend's voice wavered.

Ellie stumbled out of bed and flipped on the light. "What's going on?"

"It's on fire! The food bank building is on fire, and I'm afraid it's going to spread to Pearl's."

Ellie's heart froze. The food bank operated by Clare's husband's church was located in the building next to Pearl's Perfect Pies in downtown Pumpkinseed Lake. Ellie's Grandma Pearl had owned and operated western Wisconsin's most famous pie shop until she'd had a minor stroke a few years ago and Ellie had stepped in to run things.

She ran to her dresser and yanked open drawers, looking for something—anything—clean to throw on. She balanced the phone between her ear and shoulder and hopped on one foot while she stuffed the other into the leg of her second-best jeans. "I'll be there in ten minutes."

"Hurry!"

Ellie grabbed her parka, jammed her feet into her Sorels, and raced out to the garage. She revved up her Jeep, threw it into *Reverse*, and thanked God the town was so small. She would be downtown in ten minutes—maybe eight.

As she approached the four-block-long business district, a glow lit up the sky, interrupted by plumes of smoke. *Please don't let it reach Pearl's.*

She pulled the Jeep into an empty space at the curb a couple of blocks away and ran toward the generalized commotion, her heavy boots crunching on the packed snow with each step. Three fire trucks—the entire fleet of the Pumpkinseed Lake Volunteer Fire Department—were parked in front of the food bank. Men in heavy, soot-stained yellow suits aimed hoses at the flames shooting from the roof at the back, and a small crowd of onlookers huddled on the sidewalk nearby.

As soon as Pearl's came into view, Ellie's breathing slowed a fraction. The building stood cold and dark, ignored by the firefighters. *Thank God.* If the pie shop burned down, Ellie would be out of a job, but Grandma Pearl might never recover.

Then she spotted Clare in the waiting group and jogged toward her. Clare's long down coat barely stretched across the bulge of her tummy, and her dark hair hung in unruly ringlets beneath her knit hat. As Ellie approached, she took in her friend's pale face, swollen eyes, and reddened nose.

She reached for Clare and hugged her tight. "Everything's going to be okay. It looks like they're getting the fire under control." Scanning the onlookers, there was no sign of Clare's husband. Surely he hadn't let his very pregnant wife come out alone in the middle of the night. "Where's Karl?"

"He sh...should be here any minute. He's d...dropping Jacob off to spend what's left of the night at his parents' house. I'm s...s...sorry I woke you." Clare snuffled then pulled off one mitten and fumbled in her pocket for a tissue. She blew her nose noisily. "You didn't need to come down. The fire didn't spread to Pearl's, after all."

Ellie lifted her gaze to the top of the building, where firefighters had reduced the columns of flame to a few flickers. "No, but the food bank..."

"I don't know what we're going to do." Tears trickled down Clare's cheeks. "The shelves were stocked for the holidays. So many families depend on us."

Ellie gave her shoulders a squeeze. "Don't worry. The town will come together. We'll find a way. We always do."

A firefighter in full turnout gear approached them. When he removed his helmet, Ellie's brows drew together and her jaw tightened. Thick, black hair—curling and damp with sweat—brushed his forehead above sky-blue eyes, a crooked nose, and strong, square jaw. Tyler O'Neil, Clare's brother, the unofficial Playboy of Pumpkinseed Lake. And even better looking than the last time she saw him, if that was possible.

Ellie had known Tyler nearly all her life, but because he was four years older, she'd never known him well. To be completely honest, she'd harbored a secret crush on him for years, but she and Clare had never been more than minor annoyances, mosquitoes buzzing around the greatness that was Tyler O'Neil, Pumpkinseed Lake's favorite son—the only local puck jockey to go on to the NHL. A knee injury might have ended his playing career, but it hadn't put a dent in his local celebrity. He'd taken over the family construction business and grown it into one of the largest employers in town.

Their paths had rarely crossed in the past few years, which was fine by Ellie. The town grapevine provided more than enough information. Her friends, both single and married, carried on about Tyler as if he were God's gift to the women of Pumpkinseed Lake instead of just a retired meathead hockey player. Although she had to admit he was easy on the eyes, over the years she'd heard enough *double entendres* about his ability to put the puck in the net to make her ears bleed.

Suddenly, Ellie realized he was speaking. And she'd been staring. Heat rose in her cheeks.

71

" —think it started in the motor of one of the freezers. The rear of the building and the roof have suffered significant structural damage. The interior of the main room and the shelves are intact, but there's a lot of smoke and water damage. I don't think you'll be able to salvage much food."

"But it's only a week until Christmas," Clare moaned. "And I'm so big I can hardly move."

"I'm sure Karl and the rest of the congregation will help you pull something together." Tyler wiped the back of his hand across his forehead, leaving a pale streak in the soot. "It doesn't have to be fancy. People will appreciate anything the church can do."

"Karl is so busy right now he doesn't have a minute to spare." As Clare contemplated the smoking building, her lower lip began to tremble again. "And it's almost the end of the year. There isn't enough money in the church treasury to rebuild."

Her friend's desolation broke Ellie's heart. Clare was always so bubbly and upbeat. It hurt to see her crushed this way. "You have insurance, don't you?"

Clare sniffed and nodded. "Yes, but there's no way we can file a claim, get the money, make repairs, and re-stock the shelves in a week."

Tyler stepped forward and put his arm around his sister. "I don't want you to worry about a thing. Ellie and I will make this happen."

He called me Ellie. He hasn't said a word to me in ten years, but he remembered my name.

When he shifted his intense blue gaze to meet hers, she shivered. Maybe her friends were on to something after all. Tyler O'Neil had a way of making a girl want to say yes.

Besides, she couldn't say no to the watery hope in Clare's eyes. With orders for more than two hundred pies to fill in the next week, she had no idea where she would find time to do anything about the food bank, but she'd manage. She nodded and tried to smile. "Of course."

Clare reached for her hand and pulled her close until the three of them formed a solid unit. "You two are the best. You've never let me down."

Tyler looked over his sister's head at Ellie. "We can get together around ten at Pearl's for a strategy session." One corner of his mouth rose in a half-smile just before he winked.

She swallowed hard. What had she gotten herself into?

****

Eight hours later Tyler O'Neil parked his truck in front of Pearl's Perfect Pies. He'd spent what remained of the night mopping up the fire with the rest of the crew, dragging himself home with just enough time for a quick shower before returning to meet Ellie Markusson. A bell over the door tinkled as he entered the old brick building, and Ellie glanced up from the cash register. The tight lines framing her mouth didn't suggest she was glad to see him. Maybe she was just tired. He sure as heck was, and his knee ached like a bear.

She nodded to one of the small tables next to the front widow. "Have a seat. I'll be with you as soon as I can."

Tyler hobbled over, pulled out one of the old-fashioned bentwood chairs, and sat where he could watch her. Pearl's wasn't a restaurant, but they had a few tables for customers who wanted a slice of pie and a cup of coffee. It was smart marketing, because the tempting aromas of cinnamon and warm fruit made it impossible to walk out without wanting — no, needing — a bite, or two, or three.

He leaned back in the chair and crossed his arms while he watched Ellie greet the next customer. Her actions were brisk and efficient, her smile friendly and genuine. He hadn't paid much attention to his sister's best friend when they were growing up. The girls spent most of their time playing outside or holed up in Clare's room, giggling about some silly thing or another. If he thought about them at all, it was with annoyance. Besides, he'd spent every waking hour outside of school on the ice.

But since he'd returned to Pumpkinseed Lake, he'd noticed Ellie Markusson plenty. Fifteen years ago, she'd been a cute, snub-nosed little kid with loads of freckles. She was still petite, but now she had curves in all the right places. She wore her thick, honey blond hair in a fashionable, chunky bob, and her freckles had faded to a delicate sprinkle across the tops of her cheeks. The few times he'd tried to talk to her she'd been as prickly as a cocklebur, but then he'd never been the kind of guy to walk away from a challenge.

While he was still pondering her granddaughter, Pearl Markusson walked around the end of the counter and approached, wiping floury hands on her long white apron. Tyler started to rise, but she placed a firm hand on his shoulder. Pearl was barely five feet tall, and the white braids that encircled her head like a crown gave her an angelic air, but it was an illusion. Pearl had always been a force to be reckoned with, and her stroke hadn't changed that. She might only work a couple of hours a day now, but her presence helped keep Pearl's the local landmark it had been for nearly fifty years.

"Good morning, Tyler. What can I get you? The apple is as good as always, and the pumpkin…well, you know about the pumpkin."

He lifted a hand in a gesture of polite refusal. "Nothing for me, Mrs. Markusson. I'm just here to talk to Ellie about the food bank as soon as she gets a minute."

Pearl cocked her head and regarded him with a sharp look. "When was the last time you ate?"

He hesitated. He'd had a bowl of chili at six the night before. Was that really fourteen hours ago? It had been a long night.

Pearl didn't wait for an answer. "I'll bring you a big slice of apple raisin pie and coffee. You look like you need it."

He started to object but she had already turned and bustled off.

A few minutes later she was back with the pie and coffee, steam rising from both. Tyler swallowed and his stomach grumbled.

Pearl's faded blue eyes gleamed, and her smile held a hint of the flirtatious young girl she'd once been. "Hah! I know a hungry boy when I see one." She patted his shoulder and headed back to work.

He stabbed his fork into the flaky pastry and brought the first bite to his mouth. He closed his eyes and savored the scent of heaven. He'd eaten half the slice when Ellie appeared with a small notebook and pen in hand.

She pulled out the chair across from him and sat. "All right. Let's make this as quick as possible. I've got plenty to do, as you can see." She began writing. "I've already called the insurance company to get the ball rolling on the claim. That won't help get the food bank operational by Christmas, though." She lifted her head to meet his gaze and pressed her lips together. "I don't suppose you have any ideas about what we can do in the meantime."

Still as prickly as ever.

He wondered what it would take to change her attitude and tried a patented O'Neil smile. No dice.

He decided to set it aside for the time being and focus on the business at hand. "As a matter of fact, I do." He leaned forward and rested his elbows on the table. After we got the fire out last night, I did an inspection and inventory. With a little luck, I think we can repair the basic structure sufficiently to reopen for one day on Christmas Eve. Afterwards, they'd have to close again for a couple of months to finish the work but…" He shrugged.

She eyed him with skepticism. "That would be a blessing to the community and a huge relief to Clare and Karl, but I don't see how it's possible."

"Winter is slow season for me and my crew. O'Neil Construction will donate the labor, and I'm sure I can get Hank at the lumber yard to help with materials. It'll mean putting in long hours but we can do it."

Pearl appeared out of nowhere with another slice of pie and a cup of coffee, which she plunked down in front of Ellie. "Here. You need a break."

"You know I don't take breaks," Ellie protested.

"Maybe you need to start. Besides, it's good for business to have a cute young couple in the front window." She turned to Tyler with a smile before bustling off.

Tyler couldn't suppress a grin as Ellie frowned at her grandmother's receding back. "Pearl's a pistol, isn't she?"

When she faced him, her frown became a grimace. "Sorry about that. I love her dearly, but she gets these ideas."

He liked the way her nose wrinkled when she said *ideas*. "What kind of ideas?"

She fumbled with her notebook and pen. "The great-grandchildren kind. Now where were we?"

It was probably childish, but some unidentifiable impulse pushed him to ruffle her feathers. "What about you? Don't you want kids some day?"

"Sure, but right now we're talking about the food bank."

He speared another bite of pie. "I like kids."

"Good for you." Her tone was dry. "Now can we get back to business?"

He gave her an innocent smile. "That's why I'm here."

A tiny muscle flexed in her jaw before she returned her attention to her notes, and Tyler wondered if she was truly angry or trying not to smile.

"I'll follow up on the insurance. You'll get started on repairs." She glanced up. "But what about food for the shelves? Even if we only stock them with holiday food for one day, we'll still need enough to feed forty families. With help from the church ladies, Pearl's can bake enough pumpkin pies, but what about everything else?"

An idea swirled around and coalesced in his mind. Tyler took a swig of coffee then set the cup on the table. "I've got it covered. This is a job for the Penguins."

Ellie's soft brown brows pinched together. "The Penguins?"

"My team."

"But you're retired."

"I coach peewee hockey. My team is called the Penguins. We'll take care of the rest of the food."

She hesitated, raked him with an appraising glance, then closed her notebook. "Fine. I guess that covers it. If there's nothing else, I need to get back to work."

He had things to do, too, but found himself in no hurry to leave. "We should plan to meet again in a couple of days to touch base. Same time, same place?"

Before she could reply, two young women — girls, really — rushed toward the table.

"Tyler, it's so great to see you," one squealed.

"Are you going on the sleigh ride tonight?" the other asked, tumbling over her friend's words. "Everyone will be there."

Tyler gave her a rueful smile. "I'm afraid I have to work."

The girl's enthusiasm drained away, and her pretty young lips slid into a pout.

He sighed inwardly. He tried to be polite, but even after several years back in Pumpkinseed Lake, he still attracted an uncomfortable level of public attention. He'd grown used to it during his playing days, but how much longer would it take for people to let go of the past and accept him for what he was now?

He glanced away from the girls and realized Ellie had taken advantage of the distraction to slip away and return to the counter. When he managed to catch her eye, she froze then pointedly turned away and directed a glittering smile at her next customer — who just happened to be the town's most eligible young attorney.

Well…damn.

****

Once a player, always a player. Ellie fumed as she rang up two pumpkin pies and one mincemeat for Kora Steiglitz, the mayor's wife. *It's always the same with him.* A tiny voice in her head told her Tyler couldn't help it if females found him attractive. She shushed it immediately. She had more important concerns than Tyler O'Neil's sex appeal.

Around two o'clock that afternoon she took advantage of a lull in business to down a cup of coffee, along with a bowl of yesterday's blackberry cobbler, re-heated and topped with a dollop of whipped cream. Fortified, she gave Clare a quick call to fill her in on the meeting with Tyler. By six she could barely keep herself upright. She dragged her aching back and feet home and straight into a hot bubble bath, knowing full well she had to be back at Pearl's Perfect Pies in less than twelve hours. Her chief assistant baker would be in the kitchen by four, and Ellie usually joined her at six.

It was still pitch black when she arrived at the pie shop the next morning, but several trucks were already parked in front of the building next door. Portable lights shone through the broken windows, and the sounds of saws and nail guns filled the early morning air. The crew must be hard at work. Tyler might be a self-involved womanizer, but no one could accuse him of being lazy.

Around mid-morning a gap-toothed, red-headed boy of about eleven strode through the door with a stack of papers under one arm. He waited while she rung up a candy apple pie for Elmer McPherson, then stepped up to the counter. He pulled off his hat and one glove and thrust his hand forward. Ellie smothered a smile as she

Alison Henderson

shook his hand. He'd obviously been coached on how to present himself.

"Hello, I'm with the Pumpkinseed Lake Penguins, and we wanted to ask if you'd put one of our posters in your store." He peeled one off his stack and held it out.

She took the poster and read:

Penguin Pick-Up Food Drive
For the benefit of the Pumpkinseed Lake Food Bank
We need the following items:
Turkeys
Stuffing Mix
Canned Green Beans
Rolls
Cranberry Sauce
Members of the Penguins will stop by your home or business
to pick up donations after 1:00 p.m. on December 23rd.
Thank you for your support!

She pressed her lips together. Not a bad plan for a meathead hockey player. By enlisting the help of the whole community, they would be able to stock the food shelf in a single afternoon.

She returned her attention to the boy, who waited for her answer with a serious expression on his freckled face. "I'll be happy to help. Why don't you give me two—one for the front window and one to put here by the cash register?"

"Sure. Thanks!" The boy grinned, handed her another poster, and hustled out the front door toward the next stop on his route.

The days leading up to Christmas were always the busiest of the year at Pearl's. The bakers cranked out pies like a well-oiled machine, and Pearl put in extra hours behind the counter filling orders. This year Ellie spent every minute up to her elbows in pumpkin puree and cinnamon. Clare sent over several volunteers from the church to help, and together they filled the cooler with forty extra pies.

Ellie was almost too busy to notice the non-stop construction work going on next door. Almost. Tyler's truck was hard to miss, parked at the curb each morning when she arrived at the shop well before dawn. And she told herself she was only being civic-minded when she sent a couple of the volunteers over with hot coffee and three whole pies every morning around eleven; she had no right to be disappointed when Tyler failed to appear for the follow-up meeting he'd proposed. After all, it wasn't as if they'd made firm plans.

At nine o'clock on the morning of the twenty-fourth, Ellie left Pearl in charge of the store and rounded up three of the church volunteers to help transport the pumpkin pies next door. Although a small army of Penguins had swarmed through town gathering donations the day before, she'd kept the pies in the large commercial refrigerator at Pearl's until an hour before the food bank planned to open for business.

When she stepped through the door with the first batch of pies, she froze and sucked in a breath. She couldn't believe her eyes. It was impossible. Tyler and his crew had performed a Christmas miracle.

The charred, water-stained ceiling and walls had disappeared — replaced by fresh wood and newly-painted drywall. New glass sparkled in the old window frames, and rows of custom-made shelves and cubbies filled the back wall. Even the scarred wooden floor had received a fresh coat of varnish. And they'd done it in less than a week. Her heart swelled, and she had to blink away a sudden sheen of moisture.

Across the room, Tyler and a flock of Penguins were busy organizing the food donations and packing them into boxes that each contained the fixings for a complete family meal. Ellie had taken no more than three steps into the room when one of the boys dropped a package of stuffing mix and zoomed toward her, hands outstretched.

"Let me take those for you, ma'am."

She cringed. *Ma'am. When did I become a ma'am?* But she smiled and let him take the pies. Then Tyler glanced up and met her gaze. Her cheeks flushed at the warmth in his eyes. *Get a grip. He probably looks at every female like that.*

She stood unmoving while he finished the box he was packing and walked toward her with a smile. The temperature in the room shot up ten degrees, and she unzipped her parka. *No wonder all the women melt at his feet.*

"I want to thank you for the coffee and pie the last few days," he said. "My guys really enjoyed it. I enjoyed it, too."

Butterflies fluttered in Ellie's stomach. "Pearl always said the fastest way to a man's heart was a perfect piece of pie." She regretted the words the second they slipped out.

Tyler grinned. "Pearl was right."

The butterfly ballet became a flamenco. Unsure how to respond, she glanced around the room. "Your crew did a wonderful job with the place. I can't believe how much you accomplished in such a short time."

"Not too bad for a bunch of meathead hockey players, huh?"

Ellie's face flamed and her jaw dropped. She closed her eyes and prayed for oblivion. Surely she'd never said that in front of him.

His grin widened. "Clare told me that's what you used to call us in high school."

"I…" What could she say?

"It's okay. We probably were meatheads then."

She dropped her gaze to the floor. "My judgement might have been clouded at the time. I was only fourteen." Her voice dropped to a near whisper. "And I had a huge crush on you."

"Really?"

Shoot. He'd heard her. Why had she let that slip? She shot a nervous glance toward the door. "Um, I have to get back to the store. I'll see you around, I guess."

When she turned to make her escape, he grabbed her hand. "Hey, you can't drop a bombshell like that and run away. We've got things to discuss." She shook her head, but he tugged her hand. "Come with me. I want to show you something."

She scanned the room. Activity had halted. All eyes focused on them. The scrutiny of eight fascinated eleven-year-old boys sent chills down her spine. Time to beat a hasty retreat. "Okay."

With a firm grip, Tyler led her to a storeroom in the back. It held the piney scent of new plywood but not much else.

He pulled her loosely into his arms, and his lips curved into an amused smile. "So you used to have a crush on me."

She refused to meet his gaze. "Maybe. It was a long time ago."

He nodded and drew her closer. "We've both changed since then."

"Maybe." He'd certainly changed, or at least her opinion of him had. She used to think he was a self-centered show-off. A gorgeous, self-centered show-off, but a self-centered show-off, all the same. The past week had shown her a new Tyler O'Neil—a thoughtful, generous, hard-working Tyler O'Neil.

"You used to be cute. Now you're beautiful."

She huffed in disbelief. *Beautiful? What a bunch of…* "I don't—"

He touched a finger to her lips. "You are. I may have been a jerk in high school, but I'm trying to do better. And you may have been too young for me then, but you're not too young now."

Her insides began to melt. What was happening? She was quickly getting in over her head. Time for a distraction before the situation got out of hand. She glanced around the room. "You said you had something to show me. What is it?"

"This." He lowered his head and planted a soft kiss on her surprised mouth.

When he released her, she tried to focus on his features, but the whole world seemed askew.

"So, are you willing to give me a chance?" he asked before he kissed her again, sealing her fate.

Her head was still spinning. "Mmm" was the only response she could muster.

His lips slid down to nuzzle her neck. "I'll take that as a yes."

Ellie leaned against his sturdy chest and allowed herself to kiss him back. It was so much better than anything she had imagined as a star-struck fourteen-year-old.

The sounds of whistles and applause entered her consciousness. Her eyes flew open, and Tyler's arms tightened. Grinning Penguins and amused church ladies filled the doorway.

In the middle of them all stood Pearl. She pinned Ellie with a sharp glance, then winked. "Didn't I always tell you? Never underestimate the power of pie."

Liza's Secret Santa

Liza Tolliver turned the small package in her hands, examining it for clues. She'd found it tucked in the doorway of her shop, Tolliver's Tiny Treasures, when she'd opened the door that morning. The box was about six inches square and wrapped in brown paper. A sprig of holly brightened the simple twine bow. Next to the bow, *To Liza* was printed in pencil, followed by *From Santa*. Santa was a little early. Christmas was still a week away.

The bell above the shop door jangled and Liza looked up. Her cousin Peaches stepped into the room and stomped her boots on the mat to shake off the clumps of snow. Peaches pulled off her peach-colored knit mohair hat and unwound the matching scarf, freeing a cascade of hair the color of dark honey. Her frost-nipped cheeks were as rosy as her namesake fruit. Without thinking, Liza reached up to smooth her own dark, pixie-cut locks. Sometimes it was hard not to be jealous of her cousin. Peaches had been blessed with an abundance of. . .well, everything. She was Liza's opposite in every way — tall, blonde, curvy, and outgoing.

Oh, and engaged — can't forget that.

But Peaches was also warm, generous, and completely unselfconscious. It was impossible not to love her. They'd been best friends all the way through Little Moose Island Comprehensive School until graduation, when Liza left the island for college in Bangor and

Peaches headed off to her mother's alma mater in Atlanta.

"I'm glad you've got the heat turned up." Peaches stuffed her mittens in her pockets then rubbed her hands together and blew on them. "The wind is stiff off the harbor this morning, and it's cold enough to freeze your nose hairs."

Liza took her cousin's coat and hung it on the Victorian coat tree by the door. "The radio says there's a good chance the noon ferry will be cancelled. Thanks so much for coming out to help me."

"No problem. I love to bake gingerbread—it smells so much like Christmas—and it's for a good cause. Your giant gingerbread house will be the highlight of the church Holiday Bazaar. I can't wait to see who buys it."

"I made mountains of dough last night. It's upstairs chilling in the fridge. And I've drawn patterns for all the pieces on graph paper. If you roll, I'll cut."

"Sounds like a plan." Peaches followed Liza toward the stairs that led to her apartment on the second floor above the shop but stopped at the counter and picked up the brown-paper wrapped box. "What's this?"

"I don't know. I found it outside on the stoop when I unlocked the door a few minutes ago."

Peaches inspected the little package. "Aren't you going to open it?"

"Sure. I guess. It's probably not a bomb."

Peaches rolled her eyes. "If we had a crazy bomber on Little Moose Island, I think we'd know it. There are only three hundred and fifty people on this rock, and you and I know every single one of them—some better than we'd like."

Liza laughed and took the package. "True." She untied the twine bow and popped the tape that secured the brown paper, revealing a simple white box.

"Well, open it." Peaches made a shooing motion. "Aren't you curious?"

Liza wasn't sure what made her hesitate. After all, it was nearly Christmas. Some kind neighbor had probably made her a little treat. Maybe a piece of Mrs. Rivers' heavenly peppermint fudge. The thought made her mouth water, even though it was only nine in the morning. She lifted the lid and sucked in a breath.

This was so much better than fudge.

Atop a wad of crumpled tissue paper sat the most beautiful miniature tilt-top tea table she had ever seen. The polished mahogany top was about three inches in diameter and edged with perfectly carved pie-crust style molding, just like an eighteenth century original. Three curved legs ended in hand-carved ball-and-claw feet, complete with tiny talons. The workmanship was exquisite—easily as high in quality as any piece in her shop. It would have taken an expert craftsman weeks to create a table like this. Grandpa would have loved it.

The thought of her grandfather brought a lump to Liza's throat. Tolliver's Tiny Treasures had been his shop. In the centuries-old clapboard house on the village's cobbled main street, he'd made and sold dollhouses, furniture, and miniatures to tourists in summer and through a mail-order catalogue in winter. When Liza was growing up, she'd spent every free minute with him in his workshop or the showroom, arranging the tiny furniture in rooms and making up stories about the people who inhabited them. Tolliver's Tiny Treasures had been a magical place for a little girl with a big imagination.

After college, instead of looking for a high-powered job in Bangor or Portland as her parents had hoped, she'd returned to the island to work in the shop with Grandpa. He'd taught her the business, and she'd migrated his catalogue sales to the Internet. They'd had three wonderful years together until last summer, when he'd suffered a stroke and died suddenly. She still felt his presence every time she rang up a sale on his old cash register or sent one of his pieces to a loving new home.

The tea table reminded her of Grandpa's work — delicate and detailed. He'd patiently worked to pass on his techniques to her, but she still couldn't match his carved details and fine finishes. The tea table was an excellent example of both, its maker a true master. But who could it possibly be? She tried to conjure up likely candidates but drew a blank.

"Wow, that's gorgeous!" Peaches leaned in for a closer look. "Who do you think made it?"

Liza turned the piece in her fingers, captivated by the rich, mahogany glow of the miniature table top. "I can't imagine."

"Well, whoever it was sure must have a thing for you." Peaches grinned. "Maybe it was Rob Corbett. He had a monster crush on you in high school."

Liza snorted. "Rob's a lobsterman. His fingers are as thick as Italian sausages. He'd never be able to do work like this." She gently settled the table back in its tissue nest.

The bell over the door rang again. She glanced up as Owen Peterson stepped inside. Owen was big, blond, and as solemn as a Puritan parson. They'd known each other nearly all their lives, but he never managed more than a few words when he stopped by every day to drop off her mail. After high school, Owen had stayed on Little Moose Island to help his father and brothers at the family boatworks until he saved enough money to start his own water taxi business. He also delivered mail and belonged to the volunteer fire department. Like so many of her neighbors, he wore several hats to make ends meet and provide basic services to the residents of the island.

He waved a stack of envelopes banded inside a colorful catalogue. "I've got your mail. Any boxes to go today?"

"Yes. Over here." Liza reached behind the counter for a large bag filled with brown paper-wrapped boxes. "They're the last of my holiday orders."

Owen nodded and took the bag. "Looks like several checks in today's mail."

She smiled. "I won't turn them down, especially not at this time of year."

He didn't respond but glanced at the little tea table sitting in its box on the counter.

Peaches leaned over and picked it up. "Isn't it beautiful? It's from Liza's Secret Santa. She has no idea who it could be. Do you, Liza?"

"None at all."

Owen slowly raised his hazel gaze to meet hers and his lips twitched, but the budding smile slipped away before it began. "I better be on my way. See you tomorrow."

"Bye," Peaches called out as he left the shop, pulling the door shut behind him. She turned to Liza and shook her head. "Too bad about Owen. He's a good-looking guy but not exactly a sparkling conversationalist."

Liza nodded. She'd had a soft spot for Owen Peterson ever since he pushed Jimmy Burns down for looking up her skirt on the playground in second grade.

Owen was one of the good guys—always had been. He stood up for people who needed help. But she couldn't argue Peaches' point. "He's always been quiet."

"True. But there's quiet, and then there's silent as a sealed tomb."

Liza took one last look at his broad back as he strode past her window on his way to the bakery next door and breathed a tiny sigh. "We'd better get busy. That gingerbread house isn't going to bake itself."

****

The next morning Liza spread the baked gingerbread pieces on the kitchen table and consulted her carefully numbered diagram. She and Peaches had spent all day yesterday cutting and baking everything she needed to create a gingerbread version of Tolliver's Tiny Treasures, right down to shutters for the windows and dozens of scalloped shingles for the roof. She checked her watch. Her cousin should arrive any minute to help assemble the house.

She'd reached the main floor when Peaches blew through the door on a gust of wind.

"Ooh, it smells good in here."

Liza wrinkled her nose. "That's because you haven't been shut up with it for twenty-four hours."

Peaches hung her coat and scarf on the tree by the door. "Don't be a humbug. It's festive." When she reached the counter, her eyes lit up. "Double ooh! You got another one." She leaned over and peered into the second small box sitting on the counter next to the tea table from the day before.

"Um, hmm. First thing this morning."

Peaches lifted a perfect miniature Queen Anne style highboy from its box. "Look at the tiny drawers. They even open!" She carefully set it back. "These are both so beautiful. I hope your Secret Santa reveals himself soon. The suspense is killing me."

"Me, too. The pieces are amazing, but this whole business unnerves me."

"So your admirer is shy. I think it's romantic."

Liza rolled her eyes. "It must be the Southerner in you. You think everything is romantic." She wrapped an arm around her cousin's shoulders. "Come on, Scarlett, we'd better get to work."

As they headed toward the stairs, the bell jingled, and Owen Peterson stepped into the room.

Liza turned with a smile. "More checks today, I hope."

"Looks like it to me." It might have been her imagination, but his usually stolid expression seemed more intense than usual this morning. And when he handed her the stack of mail, his lips curved into something close to a smile.

"Look at this." Peaches pointed to the new box on the counter. "Isn't it terrific? Liza's Secret Santa has been busy."

Owen glanced down. "Very nice."

"We've been trying to figure out who it might be. You wouldn't have any idea, would you?"

Liza thought his cheeks might have grown a bit redder, but it was hard to tell under his perennial sun and wind burn. "Stop teasing the man, Peaches."

Peaches ignored her. "I thought it might be Rob Corbett, but Liza doesn't agree." She looked up into his face and all but batted her lashes. "What do you think?"

Owen muttered something under his breath.

"What was that?" Peaches asked.

"I said I'd be surprised." He turned and headed toward the door.

Liza suppressed a grin. Unlike Peaches' fiancé Greg, Owen had too much stern Yankee in him to melt into a puddle of goo whenever she channeled her inner Southern belle.

"Will we see you at the Holiday Bazaar tomorrow?" Liza called after him.

"I expect so." Then the bell jingled again and he was gone.

"I wonder what it would take to get a rise out of that man." Peaches lifted one brow. "And I wonder what would happen if you did."

Liza had wondered the same thing over the years but refused to add fuel to her cousin's speculation. "I doubt we'll ever find out, so let's get to work."

Peaches followed her toward the stairs. "You're probably right, but it might be fun trying."

Liza turned and shook her head. "Peaches Tolliver, have you forgotten your fiancé? I don't think Greg would appreciate you trying to stir up Owen Peterson."

Her cousin laughed. "Oh, I didn't mean me. I meant you. You don't have nearly enough fun. When was the last time you went on a date?"

How long had it been? Six months? A year? Longer?

"I've been busy with the shop. Besides, I've known most of the men on this island for decades. There's no excitement, no mystery."

"Owen is mysterious."

Peaches had a point. Liza had been acquainted with Owen for years but couldn't say she really *knew* him. Still, she could do without her cousin's well-meaning interference. "I don't need a matchmaker."

"I'm just saying. . ."

Liza sighed. "Let's drop the subject. Please." She started up the stairs.

"Okay." Peaches followed, humming a cheerful Christmas carol.

When they reached the kitchen, Liza turned on the burner beneath a cast iron skillet and dumped a couple of cups of sugar in the pan. "When this is melted, it will make the perfect glue to stick the pieces together."

Peaches picked up Liza's drawing of the finished design. "This house is going to be a work of art. You don't think someone would dare eat it, do you?"

"I don't know, but I want it to be safe in case someone with children buys it."

"Good idea."

As they glued the pieces together, melting more sugar when they needed it, the gingerbread house slowly took shape. By lunch time the walls and roof were firmly in place.

Liza wiped her hands on her apron, stepped back, and regarded her creation with a critical eye. "It may be a little crooked, but overall, not too bad."

Peaches sent her a look of mock disgust. "It's adorable and you know it."

It was. Grandpa would have loved seeing Tolliver's Tiny Treasures come alive in gingerbread. The thought warmed, rather than saddened her.

"It is pretty cute," Liza admitted with a satisfied smile. Then she sobered. "But now I'm worried about how to get it to the church in one piece tomorrow. I didn't realize how heavy it would be."

"Greg and I will stop by with his SUV and pick you up around one o'clock. Between the three of us, we should be able to get it safely down the stairs."

Fortunately, Greg was as generous with his time and his truck as his fiancée.

"Thanks," Liza said. "I don't think I could carry it on my bicycle."

"You know, one of these days you're going to have to break down and buy a car like a grown-up person."

"Not if I can help it. Not owning a car is one of my favorite things about living on the island. I can walk or bike everywhere I need to go."

"And if you have to carry something big like, say, a giant gingerbread house?"

Liza grinned. "That's what friends with cars are for."

Peaches returned her smile. "Naturally."

"Let's stop and let that harden before we stick the shutters and shingles on. I've got some vegetable barley soup in the fridge."

"Yum. That sounds great." Peaches untied her apron and turned on the water at the sink to wash her hands. "I'm sorry I can't stay long enough this afternoon to help with the frosting details. Frosting's my favorite part."

Liza opened the cupboard and took down a pair of blue earthenware bowls. "That's okay. I'll probably wait several hours until the molten sugar is completely cooled. I'd hate for the house to fall apart after all the work we've put in."

"You and me both. Besides, Reverend Porter would be so disappointed. She's counting on this to be a big money-maker at the Bazaar."

"I hope so."

By two-thirty, they had finished the structure of the house.

"I can't wait to see it tomorrow." Peaches pulled on her hat and wrapped her scarf around her neck.

"Thanks so much for helping me and for volunteering Greg's truck."

Her cousin stepped out on to the sidewalk and turned with a wink. "You know what they say — what's mine is mine, and what's his is mine."

"You don't know how lucky you are."

"Oh, yes, I do. See you tomorrow."

Liza closed the shop door and trudged back up the stairs to her apartment. Her feet and back ached. And it was another one of those times she struggled not to be a little jealous of Peaches. During college, her cousin had managed to find her perfect match in Greg. He was good-looking, affable, and worshipped the ground she walked on. He'd even been willing to leave Atlanta to live on a tiny island off the coast of Maine for her. If that wasn't true devotion, Liza didn't know what was.

She wondered if she would ever be so lucky. Each passing year brought her closer to thirty with no Mr. Right on the horizon. As she'd told her cousin, she knew every available man on the island all too well. Rob Corbett, the lobsterman, was friendly but dull as mud. Tony Giordano, owner of the island's only pizza parlor, was as round and soft as a ball of his own dough. Jeff Morgan owned the lumberyard and was handsome and charming but also insufferably smug.

And then, as Peaches had pointed out, there was Owen Peterson. Owen was one of those background men, the ones you never really noticed but who were always around. In Owen's case, helping others in a hundred little ways without calling attention to himself. And he was attractive in a sturdy, Viking sort of way. Maybe Peaches was right. Maybe it was time to re-think her notions about Owen Peterson.

****

The next morning Liza was in no hurry to roll out of her warm, cozy bed. She had stayed up late into the night decorating the gingerbread house. Her creation looked wonderful, but it would be a long time before she wanted to see another pastry bag. Her fingers still ached from squeezing the stiff royal icing. She'd spent hours piping designs on the shutters, defining the clapboards, and outlining each shingle on the roof. She'd even topped her masterpiece with a rooster weather vane made of marzipan.

Pushing her hair out of her eyes, she glanced at the alarm clock on the bedside table. Eleven o'clock! She hadn't slept that late since pulling an all-nighter before final exams in college. She collapsed back against the pillows. Peaches and Greg weren't due for a couple of hours—plenty of time to pull herself together. Coffee and a shower would work wonders.

By one o'clock Liza was downstairs pacing the showroom floor. She couldn't wait to get to the church. Last night she'd fallen asleep the minute her head hit the pillow, but crazy dreams about a tall, silent man had left her feeling exhausted and wired at the same time.

When Peaches and Greg arrived, he backed his SUV to the rear door and helped Liza carry the gingerbread house down while Peaches directed. As they pulled out onto Harbor Street, Liza twisted in her seat to keep an eagle eye on her precious creation. She gave up after a couple of blocks, climbed on her knees, and leaned over the back seat to grip the wooden base with both hands. Although Greg drove slowly, she flinched at every dip and bump in the road until they reached the church parking lot. If the house fell apart now after all the work she'd put into it, she might shoot herself. After a nerve-wracking trip across the icy lot and up the back steps, they eased the house onto a display table in Fellowship Hall, and she released her breath in one big huff.

Reverend Porter strode up like the former gym teacher she was, beaming at Liza as if she had scored the winning goal in the field hockey tournament. "Excellent. Excellent. Outstanding job, Liza."

Liza's cheeks warmed. "Thank you, Reverend. I hope it helps raise the money we need for the new daycare program."

"I have no doubt, no doubt at all." She pushed back the sleeve of her red sweatshirt to check her watch. "We'll give people half an hour to examine the items then start the auction."

Peaches cast a glance at the other tables, where parishioners were setting up their baked goods, needlework, and holiday crafts. "I want to look at Mrs. Needham's crocheted snowflake ornaments." She hugged Greg's arm. "I think we need some for our tree next year."

He gave her his usual good-natured smile and patted her hand. "Sure. Anything you say."

Liza smiled after them as they wandered off to explore. They were such a perfect couple. She was looking forward to her duties as maid of honor at their wedding in May.

"That's one big gingerbread house."

Her head snapped around to meet the dark eyes of Tony Giordano.

"It would look great in the window of my restaurant. Very festive, don't you think?"

She smiled. Tony was very sweet—not her type, but very sweet and unfailingly jolly. "Absolutely. You'll have to bid on it. Maybe you'll win."

"Not if I can help it." Rob Corbett stepped up to the table.

Tony looked affronted. "What would a big mutt like you do with a thing like that? It's much too beautiful for lobster bait."

Rob laughed. "I'd eat it, of course."

Liza's heart sank. She liked Rob but balked at the image of him snacking on her masterpiece.

Then Sarah Forrester poked her fuzzy, gray head around Rob's side. "I'm sorry but you're both out of luck. Arnie's whole family is coming from the mainland. I'm having thirty people for Christmas dinner, and that gingerbread house will make the perfect centerpiece."

Liza relaxed. Bless Sarah. The Forresters were her parents' oldest friends, and she would happily send her house to grace their holiday table.

Knock. Knock. Knock. Reverend Porter rapped her gavel down on the podium. "It's time for the auction. Is everyone ready?"

A chorus of *yesses* rose from the congregation.

"Then let the bidding commence!"

Liza watched from her table while item after item went to a happy new owner. Peaches beamed as she stepped away from the podium with a set of Mrs. Needham's snowflake ornaments. Finally, only the gingerbread house remained.

Reverend Porter waved her gavel in the air. "Last but not least, we have a magical gingerbread re-creation of one of our most beloved local landmarks, Tolliver's Tiny Treasures. So what am I bid for this very special, edible piece of Little Moose Island history?"

Liza warmed at the minister's words. She could almost feel Grandpa's arm squeeze her shoulders.

"Fifty dollars," Tony Giordano exclaimed then beamed at Liza.

Rob Corbett raised his hand and waved. "Seventy-five."

Tony frowned. "One hundred."

"One twenty-five."

Liza stifled a smile. If those two kept it up, the gingerbread house would raise more than she'd hoped.

"One hundred and fifty dollars." Sarah Forrester crossed her arms and sent both men a stern look.

"Two hundred," Tony challenged.

Rob's lips thinned in annoyance, but he remained silent. Tony grinned.

"Five hundred dollars," a deep voice called from the back of the room.

Heads swiveled as Owen Peterson strode toward the podium.

Reverend Porter acknowledged his bid with a tip of her chin. "That's very generous, Owen." She faced the rival bidders. "Do any of you want to top that?" Tony's dark eyes shot daggers at Owen, but he shook his head. Sarah and Rob followed suit.

The gavel came down with a bang. "Very well. The church would like to thank you for your generous donations. I hope everyone will stay for hot cider and cookies."

Owen stood before the front table with his hands shoved in his pockets, eyeing his purchase.

Liza knew she should speak to him, but she didn't know what to say. She'd never dreamed anyone would pay that much for a gingerbread house. She walked up and stood beside him. "I'll help you carry it to your truck."

He turned and almost smiled. "Do you have a ride home?"

"I came with Peaches and Greg." She glanced around but didn't see them.

"If you help me move this, I'll give you a lift."

Alone with Owen Peterson? Maybe he would open up a bit on the short ride to the shop. "Um, sure. Thanks."

It turned out Owen didn't need any help carrying the gingerbread house, but she did open the tailgate for him. After they settled the house in the back, she climbed into the cab beside him and they set off.

He seemed comfortable driving in silence, but her nerve endings began to twitch. If one of them didn't say something soon, she might have to jump out of the truck and run the rest of the way home. When they were a block away, she gulped and blurted out, "That was an amazing thing you did for the church."

He cast an inquiring glance her way but said nothing.

"Offering so much money for the gingerbread house. I know Reverend Porter was thrilled."

He shrugged. "The daycare will help a lot of people on the island. Besides, it's the best gingerbread house I've ever seen." He pulled the truck up to the back door of Tolliver's Tiny Treasures and parked.

It was too late to matter now, but Liza's curiosity got the better of her. "What do you plan to do with it?"

Owen climbed out of cab. "If you give me a hand, I'll show you."

She followed him to the back of the truck and watched while he lifted the decorated house as if it were made of spun sugar.

"Open the back door," he directed, then followed her up the steps.

After she unlocked the door, he followed her inside and carried the gingerbread house to the front showroom, where he set in on the glass counter. "Since it's a miniature version of the shop, it belongs in your front window. I'll help you make room."

She met his solemn gaze with wonder. "You spent five hundred dollars to give this back to me?"

He nodded.

"Why?"

"Like I said, it belongs here."

Suddenly an idea that had been burrowing in Liza's subconscious for several days popped to the forefront. She picked up the miniature tea table that still rested on the counter its tissue paper nest and held it in front of Owen's face. "You made this, didn't you?"

He nodded again, color rising high in his cheeks.

"Again, I have to ask, why?"

He slowly removed the table from her grasp and returned it to the box, keeping hold of her hand. "Don't you know?"

Liza's fingers tingled at his touch, her gaze holding steady. She shook her head. "Tell me."

He drew her into a loose embrace. "I've kind of had a thing for you since second grade."

Her lips curved into a smile. "A thing? What kind of thing?"

"I'm no good with words."

"You're doing fine."

"I'd rather show you."

"Go ahead," she murmured.

Then Owen pulled her hard against his chest, and brought his mouth down on hers in a kiss that released twenty years of pent-up yearning. Liza's head spun, and she held on as if her life depended on it. When he finally released her, she collapsed into him and smiled against his flannel-covered chest.

Sometimes words were overrated.

No Room at the Inn

How much wine was too much? Was such a thing even possible?

Bottle in hand, Charlene Holloway scowled at the steaming pot of Madeira sauce on the stove. As the sauce cooked down, she was supposed to add more wine, but how much? She'd been too distracted by the array of foil pans the caterer had deposited on her kitchen table to pay close attention to his instructions before he breezed out the door with a cheery, "Don't worry, it's foolproof."

It had better be.

How long had he said to re-heat the Beef Wellington? Thirty minutes or forty? And the minted carrots? Charley tipped a couple tablespoons of Madeira into the sauce then checked the pastry-wrapped tenderloin in the oven. It looked okay but what did she know? Thank heaven the guests had chosen pecan pie instead of Baked Alaska or Bananas Foster for dessert, or she might risk setting the kitchen on fire.

As owner of The Foxborough Inn Bed and Breakfast in Dobson's Ford, Virginia, Charley was used to cooking for guests. She could whip up a batch of morning glory muffins or an omelet jardinière in a wink, but a large formal dinner was well outside her comfort zone. That was why she had referred Mrs. Tisdale to Shenandoah Catering for the elaborate pre-bridal Christmas Eve dinner currently underway in the inn's dining room.

Six months ago the Tisdales had booked the entire two hundred-year-old inn for three days for their daughter's intimate, day-after-Christmas wedding. The wedding party had arrived that afternoon in a flurry of excited chatter and overloaded garment bags, and Charley and Henry, her right-hand man, had settled them in their rooms before serving sherry in the parlor. The guests were now working their way through a tureen of cream of celery soup while Charley assembled dinner plates in the kitchen.

She had just pulled the beef from the oven when something clattered against the windows, as if someone were tossing handfuls of uncooked rice against them. Sleet. Her jaw tightened. It had started—the ice storm forecasters had been predicting for days. Why did they have to pick tonight to be right?

The lights flickered, and a moment later Henry pushed open the swinging door from the dining room and poked his head into the kitchen with a look of concern on his mocha-hued face. "The guests are finishing their soup. Are the salads ready?"

Charley tossed her head to send a damp curl back where it belonged. "The plates are in the fridge. Can you serve by yourself? I'm tied up at the moment." She lifted the roasting pan with oven mitt-clad hands.

"No problem." Henry opened the wide door of the commercial refrigerator and removed the pear, walnut, and blue cheese salads. When another gust of wind flung pellets of ice against the windows, he craned his neck and peered out toward the barn with a worried frown.

The lights flickered again but regained their steady glow. "I hope the lights last through dinner."

Charley carefully transferred the Wellington to a carving board. "We'll be fine. We've got the fire going in the dining room and dozens of candles lit. If we lose power, the generator will run the furnace overnight."

Henry nodded and loaded a large serving tray with salad plates. "In the innkeeping business, it's always something. Keeps you on your toes."

That it did. In the ten years she'd owned The Foxborough Inn, she'd dealt with everything from a woman choking on the engagement ring her fiancé had placed in her champagne glass to the sheriff interrupting a wedding to haul the preacher off for fraud. Once she'd even had to fend off a flock of wild turkeys who decided to invade a tea party in the garden.

Charley held the carving knife poised above the Beef Wellington when a loud knock at the back door almost caused her to drop it. Who could that be? All the guests were accounted for, and no one in his right mind would be out in this weather. She set the knife on the table, wiped her hands on her apron, and stepped to the door. Through the small glass panes, the porch light illuminated the rugged features of a man she'd never seen before. His cap bore the logo of a building supply company, and a couple days-worth of dark beard stubbled his square jaw, not quite concealing a pair of deep creases that bracketed his mouth.

He frowned through the glass and banged again when she didn't respond. "Open up—it's an emergency!"

What kind of emergency? Before moving to Dobson's Ford, Charley had lived in Washington, D.C. long enough to learn not to open the door to a stranger without a very good reason. She leaned close to the door and peered through the window into the darkness. The man scowled, stepped aside, and thrust a teenage girl forward. The girl was small and slim but with a prominent bulge protruding between the sides of her unzipped black parka. Short, spiky, dark hair framed her thin face, and heavy mascara streaked her cheeks, whether from tears or sleet, Charley couldn't tell.

"We need a room," the man yelled through the door.

Henry appeared at her side. "What's all the fuss?"

Charley half-turned. "They want a room, but we're full up."

Henry peeked across her shoulder. "We'll figure something out. Look at that child. We can't leave her outside in this storm. It wouldn't be right. Besides, it's Christmas Eve."

Charley reached for the deadbolt and the doorknob. Henry was right, of course, and if the pair turned out to be axe murderers on the run, at least he had the old hunting rifle he used to scare off foxes from the chicken coop. She opened the door, and the man ushered the girl inside.

"Thanks." His voice was gruff as he yanked off a pair of old deerskin gloves. "The front door was locked."

"We're full and we weren't expecting anyone." Charley eyed him closely then turned her attention to the girl, who shivered and tugged at her coat with small hands clad in black fingerless gloves. They were an unlikely duo. He was tall, sturdy, and weather-beaten and looked to be more than twice the girl's age. Maybe he was her father. That would account for his sour expression. She appeared to be no more than seventeen or eighteen years old and at least seven months along.

Charley wished she could help them. Business was good, but she usually had at least one spare room for last-minute guests. Not tonight. "I'm afraid we don't have any rooms available. We're booked solid for the next two days."

The man took off his cap and slapped it against his jean-clad thigh, knocking bits of sleet onto the wide pine planks of the kitchen floor. When he raised his head, his dark eyes held a hint of desperation. "We've got to have something — anything. The roads are too bad to drive further, and I can't make her sleep in the truck." He tipped his chin toward the girl, who swayed on her feet.

"Here, child, you sit down." Henry swung a kitchen chair under her before she collapsed.

Charley sized up the situation. She had a dozen guests in the dining room who would be expecting their Beef Wellington any minute and a half-dead pregnant girl in the kitchen. Henry was dressed for serving; she had on worn jeans and an oversized gray sweater. "Henry, if you'll slice and plate the beef — the sauce is in that pan on the stove — and add the carrots from the foil pan in the oven, I'll take care of this young lady."

"No problem." He moved to the island and picked up the carving knife.

Charley opened the fridge. "I've got some soup." She turned to the strangers in her kitchen. "Do you like split pea and ham?"

"Whatever." The girl might have been going for a classic surly teenage response, but the exhaustion in her voice spoiled the effect.

The man removed his heavy brown Carhart jacket and hung it on the back of a chair. "Thanks. That sounds great. By the way, I'm Joe Matthews and this is Maria."

Charley poured the soup into a large saucepan, set it on the stove, and cranked up the gas. "Pleased to meet you. I'm Charlene Holloway, but everyone calls me Charley. Why don't you have a seat? The soup will be ready in a couple of minutes."

Joe joined Maria at the kitchen table.

Charley stirred the bubbling pot. "What brings you out in weather like this?"

"We're on the way to Roanoke," Joe replied. "My folks are expecting me for Christmas."

Just him? The girl must not be related.

Charley set two steaming bowls on the table, along with crusty chunks of French bread. "What about you, Maria?"

The girl picked up her spoon without raising her head. "I'm just on the road."

"Where are you headed?"

"Wherever. It doesn't matter. As long as it's away."

Charley sent Joe a quizzical look.

"Maria told me she's from New Jersey. I picked her up on the highway a mile or two south of Staunton. I'm a contractor there."

At that moment, the lights flickered twice and went out. Maria's spoon clattered in her bowl, but before Charley had a chance to react, the lights bloomed back to life.

Henry pushed through the swinging door, carrying the empty serving tray. "They're all set in the dining room. Before the next course, I think maybe I'd better go out and check that generator. It looks like we might be needing it."

"Take the big flashlight—" Charley pointed toward the open pantry door, "—and that slicker hanging by the door."

Henry retrieved the industrial-sized flashlight from the shelf and slipped out the back door. About ten minutes later he was back, along with a bone-chilling blast. He shoved the door closed and shrugged out of the slicker. "The generator's ready to go, but no one's going anywhere tonight. I 'bout killed myself trying to get back up the steps. There's a thick coat of ice on everything, and it's still coming down."

Charley glanced at Maria, who had almost finished her soup, then turned to Joe. "I'm so sorry, but we really don't have any rooms left. Every single bed is taken."

His dark eyes burned with resolve. "We'll take anything—even a stall in your barn if you've got extra blankets."

Charley stiffened and stood a little straighter. Was he trying to make her feel guilty? No way was she going to put a carpenter named Joe and a pregnant girl named Maria in her barn on Christmas Eve because there was no room at the inn. She'd sleep out there herself before she let that happen.

****

Joe Matthews breathed an internal sigh of relief as a look of determination settled across Charley's features. Maybe she wouldn't send them back out into the storm, after all. He hated being at someone else's mercy, even someone as pretty as Charlene Holloway, but he couldn't make the kid spend the night in his freezing truck. She was about to pass out from fatigue as it was. He glanced at Maria's drooping, dark head as she shoveled the last spoonful of soup into her mouth and noted with surprise that his own bowl was empty, too. He'd never been a big fan of split pea, but Charley's

110

soup was a nice surprise—rich and flavorful, with plenty of ham.

When she began to stack the empty bowls, he rose. "Here, let me take those."

She smiled and relinquished them. "Thanks. If you'll put these in the sink, I'll fix dessert. The plates are already prepared for the dinner guests, but I've got extra in the fridge. Do you like pecan pie?"

Pecan pie. At least one thing was going his way today. He nodded. "It's my favorite."

A pair of charming dimples bracketed Charley's smile. "Great. What about you, Maria?"

The girl shrugged. "Never had it."

Charley opened the refrigerator and removed a whole pie. "Then you're in for a treat. My pecan pie won a blue ribbon at the Virginia State Fair last year." She cut two slices and set them on the table, along with a pair of forks.

Joe slid the first bite into his mouth and closed his eyes in satisfaction. No wonder she'd won a blue ribbon—the pie was perfect, with a tender, flaky crust and firm, yet silky, filling. It might even be better than his mother's, although he'd never admit that out loud. He cast an appreciative glance her way. Besides having hair the color of rich molasses and all the right curves under her long, loose sweater, Charley Holloway was one fine cook.

"I've figured out how to solve our accommodation problem," Charley said, interrupting his bliss. "As soon as you're finished, I'll take you to my cottage out back. You can stay there."

He frowned. "But what about you? I don't want to put you out of your home."

"It won't be a problem. I've got two bedrooms."

His frown deepened as he glanced at Maria, who had nearly finished her pie. Surely Charley didn't think they were. . .

She seemed to read his mind and raised a single brow. "You can have the living room sofa."

He relaxed and picked up his fork. "That would be great. Thanks."

Ten minutes later, after retrieving their bags from the truck, he and Maria picked their way across the yard. They followed Charley to a white clapboard cottage trimmed with dark green shutters and lit by the welcoming glow of a single light on the front porch. He kept a firm grip on Maria's elbow while he helped her up the ice-covered steps. The last thing he needed was for her to fall and go into labor. He'd only known her a couple of hours, but her defensive vulnerability stirred his protective instincts.

Charley's living room was small and cozy — emphasis on the small. Joe eyed the plump flowered sofa and wondered how much of his length would fit on it. If he wanted to be able to stand the next day, he might be better off on the floor. While Charley settled Maria in the guest room and pointed out the hall bath, he took stock of the situation. He'd expected to be home with his folks in Roanoke by nightfall, not camped out on a stranger's sofa with a pregnant teenager in tow. All he wanted now was to get Maria home to his mom. She would know what to do. She always did.

When Charley walked into the room with an armful of bedding topped by a big, fluffy pillow, he reached to take it from her. "Thanks. I really appreciate this."

She glanced at the sofa with a rueful smile. "I know it's small. You might be better off in my room, and I could sleep out here."

"I'll be fine. Trust me. Your couch will be much more comfortable than my truck."

She flipped the hood on her coat back over her head. "I need to get back to the inn. I can't leave Henry to take care of a dozen guests on his own. Make yourself at home, and I'll be back in a couple of hours. You can start a fire if you want." She tipped her chin toward the neat stack of logs by the fireplace then slipped out the door.

Joe glanced at his watch. Only seven-thirty. Now what? He didn't see a television, although a well-stocked bookcase stood against one wall. He unbuttoned his coat and hung it over the back of a chair in the compact kitchen. Maybe he should check on Maria. He knocked softly on her door. Hearing no response, he turned the old glass knob and pushed the door open a few inches. The girl was fast asleep, tucked under a thick down comforter. She'd obviously washed her face and looked about five-years-old without all the mascara. He closed the door without a sound.

Maybe he should take Charley's suggestion and light a fire. Ten minutes later, with a cheery fire crackling in the fireplace, he stretched out on the sofa as best he could. It had been a long day, and it wouldn't hurt to rest his eyes for a few minutes.

He awoke suddenly to a hand shaking his shoulder and a soft, feminine voice. "Wake up."

"Huh?" He blinked and focused on Charley Holloway's face leaning over his. Almost close enough to kiss. He bolted upright, barely avoiding a collision with her chin. "What time is it?"

She laughed. "A little after nine. You're welcome to turn in, but you'll be much more comfortable if you take your boots off first."

He glanced at his feet and immediately swung them to the floor. He'd fallen asleep on a strange woman's sofa without taking his boots off. His mother would have his hide if she found out. Heat rose in his face. "Sorry."

"Don't worry about it." She set a foil-wrapped plate on the kitchen counter. "I brought the last two pieces of pie. Would you like one?"

There was never a bad time for pie, especially Charley's pecan pie. "That sounds great."

She took two plates from the cupboard. "How about a brandy? It's the perfect thing for a cold night."

He'd never drunk brandy, but a little warmth couldn't hurt. The cottage was chilly in spite of the fire. "Sure."

"It helps me unwind, although I'm not sure you need much help with that." She glanced at the sofa and her dimples re-appeared.

Joe's face warmed again, and he breathed a tiny sigh of thanks for the dim firelight. He hadn't blushed like this since high school. *What is it about her? You'd think I'd never been alone with a woman before.*

He rose and joined her as she slid the second slice of pie onto a plate and added forks. "Let me take those."

Setting the plates on the coffee table, he waited until she joined him with two juice glasses half-full of reddish-brown liquid that sparkled in the firelight.

She handed him a glass. "I hope you don't mind. The proper snifters are in the dining room at the inn."

"These are perfect. I wouldn't know a proper snifter if it bit me in the...uh, on the nose."

They sat side by side on the short sofa, eating pecan pie in companionable silence as the flames danced in the grate. After a few minutes, he took a tentative sip from his juice glass. *Yow!* The stuff burned all the way down his throat. His eyes teared and he choked.

Her dark eyes widened in alarm. "Let me get you some water."

He waved her down. "No…I'm okay…it's just that…I've never…Wow."

"It's an acquired taste. Just go slow."

He took her advice and was surprised by the warm glow that spread through his body in a matter of minutes.

She tilted her head, and her lips curved. "Better?"

He nodded. "Yeah." Blood was definitely flowing — everywhere. He shifted on the sofa. Time to re-direct his attention unless he wanted to embarrass himself further. "So, how long have you owned the Foxborough Inn?"

Her expression sobered and she stared into the fire. "I bought it ten years ago, after my parents died. I'd been working for a congressman in D.C., but their accident made me re-think my priorities. Washington's political scene lost its appeal."

Joe couldn't imagine politics ever having any appeal. "What about siblings?"

She shook her head. "I'm an only child." Her voice sounded small and lonely.

An image popped into his head of Christmas mornings with his parents, grandparents, and five siblings. Charley had likely never known that kind of cheerful pandemonium. "What do you do for holidays?"

She shrugged. "Rest. Relax."

"Alone?"

She took a sip of her brandy then nodded. "I usually close the inn right before Christmas until the middle of January. That way Henry can spend the holidays with his daughter and grandchildren."

"But not this year."

"We'll close the day after tomorrow, after the wedding party departs." She finished her drink with a final swallow and stood. "I'd better get to bed. I've got a busy day tomorrow—Eggs Benedict for twelve at nine o'clock."

Joe rose, too. "Thanks again for taking us in. I hate to add to your work."

"I don't mind. Busy is good." Her smile seemed tinged with sadness, and he wondered if it was his imagination or a trick of the shadows.

****

At six-thirty the next morning, Charley poked her nose out from under the comforter. No sound greeted her ears. Good. If she was lucky, she could grab a quick shower before her visitors awoke. Fifteen minutes later, dried and dressed, she tiptoed into the living room, where Joe Matthews' lanky form draped over her sofa in an awkward jumble of limbs and joints. He was bound to be stiff and sore when he woke up.

As if on cue, Joe rolled over and groaned. He scrubbed his prickly face with one hand then ran it through his hair. When he shoved the blanket aside and pushed to his feet, Charley winced.

"Sorry," she said.

He made a wry grimace. "I may never walk again."

"There are fresh towels in the bathroom. You'll feel better after a hot shower."

As he stumbled down the hall, she smiled and began humming a little tune under her breath. It had been ages since she'd seen a man first thing in the morning. It was kind of nice.

When he returned, dressed in clean clothes and sporting a fresh shave, she directed him to the kitchen table. "Sit."

He sniffed the air and his expression perked up. "Yes, ma'am."

"Eat." She set a heaping plate of French toast and bacon in front of him.

"You didn't have to do this," he objected, picking up his fork. "It's too much work." The last bit came out muffled by a mouthful of food.

She couldn't suppress a little buzz of gratification. Apparently her cooking was good enough to make a Southern boy forget his manners. "I enjoy cooking breakfast. It's my favorite meal."

"Morning."

Charley turned as Maria appeared in the doorway, wearing flannel pajama pants with koala bears and a long t-shirt that stretched tight across her tummy. She looked heart-breakingly young.

"Have a seat and I'll bring you some French toast. Do you like bacon?"

Maria gave her a classic teenage *duh* look. "Who doesn't like bacon?"

Charley smiled. "Exactly."

Joe finished his breakfast as Maria dug into hers. He rose and picked up his dishes. "Have you checked the weather this morning?"

Charley pushed back the lace-edged curtain over the sink. "The sleet stopped sometime during the night." She leaned forward on tiptoe to check the thermometer mounted to the outside of the window frame. "It's already above freezing. The roads will thaw in an hour or two."

117

Joe's arm brushed hers as he peered out the window. "Then we shouldn't have any trouble making it to Roanoke in time for Christmas dinner with my folks."

Maria's chair scraped the floor as she jumped up with a speed that belied her belly. "We gotta go now." Her eyes darted between Charley and Joe, and urgency vibrated in her voice.

Joe crossed the room and laid a big hand on her shoulder. "Hey, it's okay. We've got plenty of time."

Maria shook her head. "No, you don't understand."

"Understand what?"

"We gotta go. They'll catch me." She spread a protective hand across her belly.

The girl was clearly terrified.

Charley hurried to Maria's side, slid her left arm around the girl's back, and placed her hand over Maria's, holding her in a loose embrace. She frowned when the girl's icy hand twitched beneath hers. "You're freezing." She lifted her gaze to meet Joe's, and he nodded and strode to the fire to toss on a couple more logs.

Charley guided Maria to the sofa. "Everything's going to be fine. Come sit and warm up. Then you can tell us all about it." Maria shook as Charley plucked the rumpled blanket off the sofa and wrapped it around her shoulders before sitting beside her.

Joe dragged a chair over and sat, taking her hands in his. "Maria, I won't let anyone hurt you. Trust me."

"You d-don't even know me."

"I know you need help. That's enough."

"Who do you think is after you?" Charley asked quietly.

Maria drew a shuddering breath. "Big Sammy, or a couple of his guys. He probably wouldn't do something like that himself."

Joe stroked her hand with his thumb. "Something like what?"

"He wants to make me disappear." She shivered. "Because of the baby, you know."

Charley glanced at Maria's belly. "Is that Big Sammy's baby?"

Maria jerked upright and wrinkled her nose. "Eww, no. Big Sammy is, like, old. It's Little Sammy's."

"His son?"

"Yeah."

"I'm sure this man wouldn't harm his own grandchild."

Maria tossed her spiky black cap of hair. "Hah! You don't know Big Sammy Spitelli. When he wants someone disappeared, they disappear."

Joe sat back in his chair. "Well, you're not going to disappear."

"Then we gotta get out of here. Big Sammy's guys have been following me for three days in a black Cadillac with dark windows. That's why I had to get out of Jersey."

Joe planted his hands on his thighs and pushed up. "In that case, we should be able to safely hit the road by nine. You finish your breakfast and take a shower, and I'll go out and start chipping the ice off the truck."

"I'll walk with you." Charley stood. "I've got to get breakfast started for the wedding party. Maria, don't you worry. You're going to be fine." She pulled on her coat and followed Joe out the door.

The ice storm had transformed the inn and its surroundings into a glittering wonderland. Even the barn looked like something out of a fairy tale. The *drip, drip, drip* of water filled the early morning stillness as tiny icicles melted on the eaves and gurgled through the gutters and downspouts.

Charley caught up to Joe in a few paces. "What do you think of her story?"

"It doesn't matter what I think. She's scared, so I'll get her to Roanoke as soon as possible."

"What will happen then?"

"I don't know, but my mom's a retired social worker. She knows people who can help."

Just then the crunch of tires on the ice-covered gravel driveway drew Charley's attention as a vintage black Cadillac drove slowly toward the inn. She and Joe stood frozen as the car disappeared around the front of the building. Then a door slammed, followed quickly by a second.

Joe muttered an expletive and started forward, but she laid a hand on his arm. "Go back to the cottage and help Maria get ready to go. I'll take care of this."

She left him and scurried up the slick back steps. This was her inn, and nothing bad was going to happen here on Christmas Day. Period.

Dumping her coat in the kitchen, she took a deep breath and marched down the short hall, past her office, to the lobby. Henry must have risen early and unlocked the front door. He'd also turned on the lights on the Christmas tree. The cheerful, multi-colored sparkles were a stark contrast to the three men in black wool overcoats who stood in front of the desk, stomping their feet and rubbing their hands together. When they saw her, they stilled.

Charley lifted her chin and pasted a smile on her face. "Merry Christmas. What can I do for you gentlemen?"

The tallest stepped forward. "We're traveling with some friends—a man and a girl. We got separated last night because of the weather and wondered if they stopped here."

"The girl's knocked up," the short, round one added helpfully. "You can't miss 'er."

"I'm sorry, but I can't help you. All our rooms are occupied by a wedding party."

The tall one eyed her closely and twisted a chunky gold ring on his right pinky. "You sure you haven't seen them? They were headed this way. We're in the freaking middle of nowhere here. There's no place else to stop for miles. We had to sleep in the freaking car."

The medium-sized man tugged on the tall one's sleeve. "Vinnie, if they're not here, they're not here. We better get going and find them. Big Sammy's not gonna be happy."

Jeez. Could these guys be for real? They looked and sounded like extras from *The Sopranos.* But what did she know? She'd never been to New Jersey.

Vinnie pursed his lips for a moment. "Right. Let's go."

Charley glanced at the grandfather clock across the lobby and chewed her lip. What if Maria was right? What if Vinnie and his pals really were some kind of Mob enforcers? She wished she knew if Joe and Maria were still in the cottage. She didn't want these goons to leave now and run into them outside. She needed to stall Big Sammy's men long enough to give Joe and Maria a good head start.

"I'm about to start breakfast for my guests. Can I fix you gentlemen something before you go? You might have a long, cold drive ahead of you. I doubt any place else will be open Christmas morning."

"No, thanks. We need to be going." Vinnie started to turn toward the door, but his short associate stopped him with a tug on his sleeve.

"We got time, and we gotta eat. I'm starved, and like you said, there's no place else around for miles."

"I'm making Eggs Benedict," Charley added.

The three faced her and then each other. She held her breath.

Finally Vinnie relented. "Okay, but you guys need to eat fast."

His cohorts readily agreed, and Charley ushered them into the kitchen and seated them at the table. On her way to the fridge, she glanced out the window and saw Joe's truck still parked near the barn. Her stomach began to churn. What if one of the men spotted it? If they knew Joe and Maria were together, they must know the kind of vehicle he drove.

However, the men quickly became embroiled in conversation about someone named Sal who owed Big Sammy money over a failed business deal and what they were going to do about it. Charley tuned them out and concentrated on getting food in front of them as quickly as possible. They were less likely to notice anything happening outside with her Eggs Benedict under their noses.

Ten minutes later she poured herself a cup of coffee and leaned one hip against the sink. The only sounds coming from the table were grunts of satisfaction as the men concentrated on their food. Something dark along with a flash of movement outside caught her attention. She shot a quick glance out the window to see Joe helping Maria across the icy yard to his truck. Her heart pounded in her throat. How far would the sound of the doors closing carry in the still morning air? She needed to create a distraction, but what?

Music. There was a CD of holiday favorites in the player in her office and speakers throughout the first floor. Perfect. She set her cup on the counter and headed toward the door.

As she passed, Shorty twisted in his chair, raised his cup, and looked over his shoulder in the direction of the window. "Could I have another. . .Hey, Vinnie, isn't that the girl?"

The next seconds passed in a blur. Shorty dropped his cup, sending porcelain shards across the floor. All three men jumped up, knocking over their chairs in haste to reach the door. Charley picked up the closest weapon she could find—a broom—and chased them down the slippery steps as they raced toward the truck, yelling all the way.

As they neared the truck, Joe cranked the engine and slammed it into *Reverse*. The men jumped back, and Charley plowed into Shorty, knocking them both to the ground. Tires squealing, the truck shot backward about twenty feet then lurched to a stop as a hulking black Escalade blocked its path. When Joe tried to pull forward, Big Sammy's men boxed him in.

Charley halted, broom in hand. She needed to call the sheriff, but her phone was still in the cottage. What were the chances she could slip away unnoticed? She took one step backward, then another. Just when she was about to make a run for it, the doors of the Escalade flew open and two men jumped out. The driver was short, stout, and middle aged, and his passenger was the exact opposite. The gangly young man sprinted to the truck and yanked open the passenger side door.

Vinnie ran to meet the driver. "Boss, what are you doing here?"

"What I should have done last week, instead of sending you three jokers."

"But we found the girl, just like you told us. We were bringing her back." Vinnie's voice held a pleading note.

Charley clenched her teeth and tightened her grip on the broom. There was no time for the sheriff. She would have to handle the situation herself. This was her inn, and she was not going to have a Mob hit in her back yard on Christmas morning. End of story.

She shoved Shorty aside and marched toward Big Sammy. "You there, what are you doing here?"

Big Sammy furrowed his brow. "Who are you?"

"I own this inn, and you and your associates are not welcome. I'll thank you to leave immediately."

"Look, lady. We got no beef with you. We'll leave as soon as we get what we came for."

Joe had climbed from the truck and approached the group with a small sledge hammer clutched in one fist.

Big Sammy jerked his chin in his direction. "Tell the big guy to drop the hammer. We don't want to make trouble. We're just here to pick up —"

The tall, skinny young man appeared from the other side of the truck with one arm wrapped around Maria's shoulders and a worried look on his face. Tears leaked from her non-mascara'ed eyes. "Pop, I told you not to send Vinnie and the boys. They've scared her half to death."

Big Sammy strode over to the young couple and reached for Maria's hand. She hesitated then proffered it reluctantly before snuggling back into the safety of Little Sammy's embrace.

He leaned toward her. "Young lady, you are one slippery customer. The boys have been looking for you for three days."

"I know," she acknowledged in a small voice. "That's why I ran."

"I bet you don't know I sent them to bring you to the house to spend Christmas with the family."

"B-but you hate me."

"Nah. At first, maybe I wasn't too pleased when Little Sammy told me he was gonna be father. But eventually, the missus, she. . .uh. . .helped me see the error of my ways."

Little Sammy grinned. "Ma chased him around the kitchen with a rolling pin, yelling at the top of her lungs that nobody was gonna deprive her of her first grandbaby."

His father grimaced. "So, Maria, are you willing to let bygones be bygones and become a member of the Spitelli family?"

She glanced up at Little Sammy's adoring face. "Sammy's gotta ask me himself."

The young man promptly dropped to one knee on the crunchy grass and took her hands. "Maria Bartoli, will you marry me?"

She smiled and nodded. "I guess."

Big Sammy smiled and rubbed his hands together. "Good. That's settled. Let's get going. Mama's got Christmas dinner in the oven, and if we're late, she'll make minestrone out of me."

Joe stepped forward. "Maria, are you sure you want to go with them? You don't have to, you know." He slapped the hammer against his palm.

The girl pulled away from her fiancé's arms and went to Joe. Standing on tiptoe, she planted a swift kiss on his cheek. "I want to. Don't worry. And thanks for taking care of me."

Two minutes later, Charley stood in the yard staring at receding taillights. "What just happened? I feel like I've been part of some ridiculous reality TV show."

"That makes two of us."

"It was kind of sweet, though."

Joe nodded.

Out of habit she glanced at her watch. Eight o'clock had come and gone.

Yikes!

She tamped down the rising panic and turned to face him. "I'm sorry to run, but I've got to serve breakfast for twelve in half an hour." She stuck out her hand. "It was nice to meet you, even under such bizarre circumstances. Have a safe trip home and Merry Christmas."

Instead of the quick, friendly shake she'd intended, he held her hand a bit longer than necessary then gave it a squeeze before releasing it. "I just had a thought. How would you like to come home with me for New Year's?"

Charley's brows pinched together. Had she heard him correctly? She liked Joe and he was certainly attractive, but they hadn't even known each other twenty-four hours.

His dark eyes sparkled with seductive mischief. "When I called home, I didn't give my mom any specifics about Maria—I didn't want to worry her—but when I told her I was bringing a girl home for the holidays she was pleased. . .and more than a little relieved, I think. She's been after me for years about the state of my social life. I'm sure she'd be happier to see you than a pregnant, Goth teenager."

Hearing the love in his voice when he talked about his mother brought an ache to her heart and a lump to her throat. "It's not that I don't want to make your mom happy, but—"

His expression sobered. "It would make me happy. I could stay and help out here until your guests leave. Then we could drive to Roanoke together. A few days of R & R would do you good. You look tired."

Ouch. Not exactly what a girl wants to hear from a good-looking guy. "Gee, thanks."

"Tired, but beautiful. I'm just saying you could use a little spoiling."

Was he trying to melt her like last week's snowman? Nobody had spoiled her, or even suggested it, in years, and if they had, she would have rebuffed them. She'd made her own way and forged her own life since her parents' deaths. She had the inn. She had Henry for help. She was in control. It was a safe life.

"You'd love it," he continued. "One of my sisters and her husband host the annual family New Year's Eve party, and my mom makes killer black-eyed peas the next day."

Family, a party, and the opportunity to eat someone else's cooking. Her walls began to crumble. He seemed to know just how to hit her soft spots.

"Come on." His lips curved up in a teasing half-smile. "Take a chance."

Should she? Could she? She hadn't had a reason to celebrate the beginning of a new year in ages. Maybe it was time. She drew a deep breath then released it. "Okay. Yes, I'd like that."

Joe's smile widened, and his eyes sparked. "You won't be sorry."

Charley tipped her head and met his warm gaze. "You know, I don't think I will."

Second Hand Hearts

Rachel Corbin bit her tongue as she slipped in a small puddle of Chihuahua pee. Again. One glance at Pepe's guilty face confirmed her suspicion. If Violet Marsdan insisted on bringing her pet along for her weekly volunteer shifts at Furry Friends, why couldn't she remember to walk him first? Since the shop operated as a benefit for the SPCA, most pets were welcome, but Pepe really pressed his luck.

"Violet—"

The plump, middle-aged woman blushed and grabbed a paper towel from behind the front desk. "I'm so sorry. He gets excited every time we come here."

Rachel shook her head as Violet wiped up her precious pooch's piddle. Again. It seemed neither Violet nor Pepe was capable learning from experience. Fortunately, the shop had a tile floor.

"She needs to give that dog a Valium."

Rachel grinned as she turned to the diminutive woman at her side. Trudy Mayfield was a real character and one of Furry Friends' most stalwart volunteers. She'd worked at the shop long before Rachel had been hired as manager seven years ago. Today Trudy was helping her mark a new batch of donated china knickknacks for sale.

"I love animals, but I don't know why anyone would want a neurotic little yipper like that around," Trudy muttered.

Rachel silently agreed but didn't want to alienate Violet. Furry Friends depended on reliable volunteers. "I'm sure Pepe is a good companion."

"Hmmph. Makes me nervous just to look at him."

"Well you know what they say, different strokes for different folks."

Rachel had met Trudy's deceptively placid Maine Coon cat Boris once when the two had stopped by the shop on the way to the vet. If he were so inclined, Boris could take Pepe out with one swipe of his enormous paw. Since Trudy was barely four foot ten, Rachel had always wondered about the pet/owner relationship in that house.

Trudy regarded the gaudy Christmas sweater in her hands with a critical eye before marking the tag two dollars. "So, Rachel, do you have big plans for this evening?"

The question caught her off-guard. It had been ages since she'd had big plans for any evening—especially since David left. Had it really been five years? Maybe her New Year's resolution should be to get out more. "Nope. No big plans."

"Do you think you could leave a bit early today and give me a ride home? The Senior Bus is booked solid with a holiday lights tour group, and there's something I'd like to talk to you about."

I wonder what she's got in mind this time. Trudy's ideas were legendary. A few years ago she'd decided the parking meters on Ocean Boulevard were unfriendly to locals and visitors alike. After she commandeered the agenda at a closed-door city council meeting, the meters mysteriously disappeared under cover of darkness. No public official ever spoke of it again.

Rachel nodded. "Sure. I can be ready around four o'clock."

They worked another couple of hours receiving new donations, sorting, and pricing, leaving Violet and Pepe to man the cash register. A few minutes after four, Rachel collected her purse, zipped her quilted jacket, and shepherded Trudy to her little Honda in the parking lot of the shopping center that housed Furry Friends. She shivered as swift gray clouds blew in from the ocean on a chilly breeze. As soon as she started the car, she cranked on the heater.

"That feels good on these old bones." Trudy rubbed her arms.

"Well, it is only a week until Christmas. The weather was bound to turn, even in Cypress Cove."

"At least it's not raining. Back in Massachusetts, where I grew up, they're up to their eyebrows in snow."

Rachel nodded, keeping her eyes on the winding highway. "Coastal California is pretty close to paradise. I even enjoy the energy of a wild winter storm from time to time."

Trudy snorted. "If you come out to my house during the next big blow, you might change your tune."

Trudy and her late husband, legendary film director Clyde Mayfield, had bought Casa de las Olas — House of the Waves — early in their marriage as a retreat from the hectic pace of Hollywood. The 1920's era, Spanish-style house hugged the rugged coastline of the highlands a few miles south of Cypress Cove. Rachel had never been inside, but she could imagine angry winter waves crashing against the rocks, tossing spray against the leaded glass window panes.

When they reached the imposing wrought iron gate, Trudy gave her the security code. The gate swung open then closed behind them as they drove down the driveway paved with crushed abalone shells. Rachel parked in front of the house then went around to help Trudy out of the car.

The older woman fumbled briefly in her purse for her keys before unlocking the massive oak door, which was decorated with black wrought iron studs. She shoved the door open with her shoulder and muttered, "I'm not going to miss this."

Rachel wondered what she meant, but it didn't seem polite to ask. She followed Trudy into the tiled foyer and froze. Three wide steps led down to a large, sunken living room with a wall of windows, each framing a spectacular view of the Pacific.

Trudy set her purse on a carved antique console table. "Come into the kitchen and I'll fix us a cup of tea. There's a nice spot in the study where we can watch the sunset."

A few minutes later, Rachel carried a tray with a flowered teapot, two cups, and a plate of Christmas cookies into a room dominated by floor-to-ceiling bookshelves crammed with books, knickknacks, and Hollywood memorabilia. A heavily carved wooden desk held court in the center.

A nostalgic smile lit Trudy's face. "This was Clyde's inner sanctum. He worked a lot of big deals from that desk. I mostly use it as a TV room now. You can set the tray over there." She pointed Rachel to a small round table with two chairs near the window. A long-haired tabby cat with lynx-like ears completely filled the seat of one chair. His eyes glowed molten gold, just as Rachel remembered.

"Hey, Boris." She bent down to scratch his ears. Boris let out a rumble and raised his chin to be scratched.

"Boris, get down," Trudy commanded. He merely blinked and began washing a paw.

"He can sit on my lap," Rachel offered. "I love cats."

"I wouldn't recommend it. Your legs would go numb. He weighs almost twenty-five pounds. Boris, I said get down." Boris gave Trudy another slow blink then rose, stretched, and hopped to the floor with a thud.

Rachel smiled. "Looks like you won that round."

"I always do. I think he knows I can't pick him up anymore and takes pity on me."

Boris strolled across the room and levitated effortlessly onto the top of Clyde's desk. From his new domain, he stared without blinking while Trudy poured two cups of tea. As Rachel sipped the cinnamon-flavored brew, she couldn't keep from sneaking peeks at the furniture and accessories sprinkled around the room. Casa de las Olas was a veritable treasure trove. With a degree in art and seven years' experience managing a benefit shop in one of the wealthiest communities on the coast, she had an eye—if not the budget—for beautiful things.

"Your home is lovely."

"I'm glad you think so." Trudy gave a brisk nod. "That's why I invited you here. I need your help."

Rachel set her cup in its saucer. Trudy had frequently mentioned the women who cleaned her house every other Tuesday, and Rachel had met Manuel, the gardener. What additional help did she need? It didn't really matter—she would be happy to lend a hand wherever she could. Over the years, the older woman had become a good friend. "What can I do?"

"I've decided to sell the house."

Even though Rachel had never been inside Casa de las Olas before, Trudy's announcement sparked a pang of regret. She couldn't imagine the house with a new owner. Each room bore the Mayfields' stamp. Sixty years of memories filled every corner.

Trudy titled her head and pursed her lips. "I'm not getting any younger, you know. I'll be ninety next month."

Rachel blinked in disbelief. *Ninety? Impossible.* Trudy had always run circles around the other volunteers at Furry Friends. She might have slowed a bit in the last few years and perhaps shrunk an inch or two, but she couldn't be ninety. Not Trudy.

"Is there something I can do to make it easier for you to stay?"

The older woman shook her head. "No. My mind's made up. Clyde and I loved it here, but it's too much house for me—has been for years."

"Where will you go?" Rachel hoped Trudy planned to stay in the area. She couldn't imagine Cypress Cove or Furry Friends without her.

Trudy's faded blue eyes crinkled, and she reached over to pat Rachel's hand. "Don't look so distressed, dear. I've signed up for an apartment at Cypress Manor. Most of my friends live there, and I want to make the move while I still have plenty of zip. I'm excited."

Cypress Manor was a lovely, upscale retirement home on the outskirts of Cypress Cove. The decision made sense, and it was so like Trudy to take control of her own future rather than force her family to make difficult decisions for her later.

Rachel squeezed her friend's hand. "Then I'm excited for you. How can I help?"

Trudy cast a glance around the room. "You can help me decide what to do with all this *stuff*. I want to take some of the special things with me, and I'm sure Joe and Carol and the boys will want a few family mementos, but that still leaves an awful lot of *stuff* – some of it possibly quite valuable by now." She returned her gaze to Rachel. "You know about these things. You can help me decide what to sell and what to donate."

Excitement quickened Rachel's pulse. Trudy's proposal would be a challenge. Her studies hadn't prepared her to evaluate all the Mayfields' treasures, but she loved research. "I'll do my best, and I'm sure we can locate experts to call on when we need them."

Trudy dipped her chin in a nod of approval. "That sounds like an excellent plan. How soon can you start?"

Rachel retrieved her phone and checked her calendar. "How about Wednesday evening?"

Before Trudy could answer, a door slammed somewhere in the back of the house. They both started and Rachel gripped her phone. She was sure they'd been alone in the house. Had someone broken in? She started to press nine-one-one.

"Grandma!" a deep, masculine voice called from somewhere in the vicinity of the kitchen.

Trudy relaxed and smiled. "It's Mark."

Moments later a man appeared in the doorway. Rachel hadn't seen Mark Mayfield since high school, where he'd been a couple of years ahead of her. He still had the tall, lanky build and sandy hair she remembered, but an overlay of sophistication had replaced his earnest, adolescent geekiness. The expensive haircut didn't hurt, either. The president of the math club had grown into a very attractive man.

With grandmotherly pride, Trudy had kept Rachel apprised of Mark's activities over the past few years, so she knew he and a college buddy had founded a frighteningly successful tech company in Silicon Valley several years ago. She also knew he'd gone through an ugly divorce last year when his wife left him for his business partner. When he stepped into the room, the light cast his features into sharp contrast, etching lines of exhaustion around his eyes and bracketing his mouth.

Trudy beamed. "Mark, come in, come in. What a wonderful surprise! Why didn't you tell me you were coming down?"

As he approached the table, he seemed to notice Rachel for the first time, and his brows drew together. "It was a spur of the moment decision." He bent down, slid one arm behind his grandmother's back, and pressed a kiss to her forehead.

Trudy clasped his free hand between hers. "You remember Rachel Corbin, don't you?"

****

Mark's frown deepened. The woman across from his grandmother looked familiar, but he couldn't place her. Her classic California look—shoulder-length blond hair with subtle highlights and dark blue eyes—was spoiled only by a nose a little too long to be plastic-surgeon perfect. Her name sounded familiar. Rachel Corbin. Oh, yes—the woman who ran the thrift shop where Grandma volunteered. He usually tuned his grandmother out when she chattered on about *Rachel this,* or *Rachel that.* What was she doing here?

The last thing he needed was a stranger in the house. He hadn't slept in two days, his eyes burned, and his head hurt. He'd driven two hours through crazy, bumper-to-bumper traffic from San Jose, desperate for the peace and comfort of home. Even though it had been twenty years since he and his brother had lived with Grandma while their parents ran an archeological excavation in the Mayan jungle, Casa de Las Olas would always be home. The House of Waves — even the name soothed his frazzled nerves.

Now, he just wanted Rachel whatever-her-name-was to leave so he could grab a quick shower and collapse into bed in his old room. He might not come out for a week.

"Can you stay the weekend, dear?"

Mark glanced down at his grandmother's upturned face and nodded. "Maybe even longer."

In fact, he didn't know when, or if, he could bring himself to face Leon Margoles again. They'd been best friends since their first week of college and had joined forces to found El Dorado Technologies soon after graduation. Their friendship had ended when Calisa left him and moved in with Leon. For the sake of the company and its employees, Mark had managed to maintain a professional demeanor at work, but the effort had taken an increasing toll since the divorce last year. Then yesterday morning he'd received an invitation to Calisa and Leon's wedding. His fortitude had crumbled.

"It would be wonderful if you could stay through Christmas, or even New Year's." His grandmother's voice intruded on his thoughts. "I can't remember the last time you took a vacation."

Neither could he. "I might be able to work that out." He kissed her forehead a second time and straightened. "Right now, I'm beat."

"Here, have a cookie to tide you over." Grandma handed him a snowman-shaped sugar cookie with a red frosting scarf. "If Rachel will give me a hand in the kitchen, we can whip up tomato soup and grilled cheese sandwiches. I know they're your favorites. You can have a quick supper and turn in early."

"That's—"

"I really have to—"

He and Rachel spoke simultaneously then stopped.

Grandma pushed back from the table and rose, using the arms of the chair for leverage. "No arguments. It'll only take a few minutes." She pinned Rachel with a gaze. "You said you didn't have plans this evening."

A becoming blush rose in the pretty blonde's cheeks. "I don't."

Then Grandma turned her eagle eye on him. "And you're practically dead on your feet. Sit here. Boris will keep you company. We'll be back with supper before you know it. And try to stay awake, dear."

Only a fool argued with Trudy Mayfield, so he sat. She patted his hand then headed for the kitchen with Rachel in tow. As if on cue, Boris roused himself, stretched, and hopped down from the desk. He ambled over to stand at Mark's feet and yowled.

"Hello, Boris."

Grandma had adopted Boris five years ago after her elderly Cocker Spaniel passed on, and Mark had never developed much of a rapport with the cat. Frankly, it was hard to relax in the company of an animal that looked like a small bobcat. They eyed each other with suspicion until Boris gave another loud *meow* and hopped up on Mark's lap. After a few seconds, he tentatively stroked the cat's ears and was rewarded by a loud, rumbling purr. Wrapped up in his thoughts and lulled by the warm, vibrating weight on his lap, he started when Grandma and Rachel re-appeared with a tray filled with three steaming bowls and a platter of golden grilled cheese sandwiches cut on the diagonal, just the way he liked them.

Rachel pulled up another chair, and they began to eat. From time to time Boris head-butted Mark's elbow, demanding bites of sandwich, so Mark complied. If he wanted to stay at Casa de las Olas for a while, he didn't want to risk getting on Boris's bad side.

After a few minutes, Grandma set her spoon aside and regarded him with a tiny frown. "Before you arrived, I was telling Rachel I've made a big decision about the house."

A decision? About the house? That sounded ominous.

"I'm going to sell Casa de las Olas and move to Cypress Manor after my birthday next month."

Mark's stomach lurched as if he'd been standing on the edge of a cliff and the earth vanished beneath his feet.

Grandma reached for his hand. "Don't look like that, dear. We all knew this day had to come."

He hadn't known. He'd never even considered it. Grandma had always been his rock. This house was home.

"Rachel has agreed to help me sort through the furniture and things and decide what to sell and what to donate."

He dropped his forehead into one hand, as if that would stop the reeling. His life was spinning out of control. He'd come to Cypress Cove for solace and comfort, only to have it ripped away.

A kernel of anger ignited in his belly. It must be her doing, this Rachel Corbin. Who was she, anyway? She must have talked Grandma into selling the house so she could get her hands on its treasures for that shop she ran, or maybe earn a commission selling them outright. Well, that wasn't going to happen.

As he shoved back from the table and started to rise, Boris's claws dug into his thighs. He bit back a curse as the cat leapt to the floor. "I can't think now. We'll talk about this tomorrow. I've got to get some sleep."

"That's a good idea, dear. Tomorrow will be soon enough."

****

The next afternoon, Rachel hesitated as she stood on the front porch of Casa de las Olas with her finger poised over the doorbell. Trudy had called and asked her to come by to begin preparing an inventory of the contents of the house, but she was nervous about seeing Mark. Trudy had insisted he had accepted her decision, but Rachel had seen the burning suspicion in his eyes before he stomped out of the room the evening before. He didn't like her, he didn't trust her, and she didn't know why.

It would be great if she and Mark got along—he was attractive, intelligent, and successful. But ultimately it didn't matter. Trudy was her friend and had asked for her help. She would brave the lion's den for her friend. She drew a deep breath, screwed up her courage, and rang the bell.

Mark Mayfield answered the door. His sandy hair was tousled, his feet were bare despite the December chill, and his shirt hung open to reveal a gray tee shirt that read *Nerds Rule*. On the surface he looked like the embodiment of a bad hangover. But his eyes looked clearer. The shadows had faded and the lines relaxed. The angry desperation had dissipated.

"Hi," he said.

Rachel eyed him warily. "Hi."

He swung the door wide and stepped back. "Come on in. Grandma's waiting for you in the study."

She didn't need an escort since she was now familiar with the layout of the house, but he trailed along beside her.

"I've been talking to Grandma."

Rachel kept her focus straight ahead. "That's good."

"She really wants to move."

"That's what she said, and in my experience, she always means what she says."

He reached for her arm. "Hang on a minute."

She stopped and pinned him with a pointed gaze.

He immediately released her arm. "Sorry. I just wanted to talk to you a minute, to apologize."

"And you have."

He scrubbed a hand over his unshaven jaw and up through his hair. "I wasn't at my best last night. I was rude and abrupt. I know it's no excuse, but my life has been a mess lately."

At the unspoken plea in his hazel eyes, the knot in Rachel's chest loosened. "Trudy told me. It's okay — really."

"No, it's not okay, as she pointed out to me this morning."

Rachel had never been on the receiving end of a Trudy Mayfield tongue lashing, but she could easily imagine. Trudy always said she was too old to waste time beating around the bush.

"Despite what she says, I'm sure the thought of moving is stressful for her."

"You're probably right." Twin grooves appeared between his brows. "It's sure as hell stressful for me."

"If you have room at your place, you should choose a few mementos from the things Trudy can't take with her. I know that's what she wants."

Mark considered a minute then nodded. "I will."

Rachel offered her hand with a tentative smile. "Maybe we can work together to help make Trudy's transition as easy as possible."

When he took her hand, his grip was firm and warm, but not too tight. Strength radiated down to the fingers clasping hers, but he wasn't trying to intimidate or overpower her.

"Agreed." He held her hand a beat longer than necessary, then released it before leading the way into the study where Trudy sat on the green velvet loveseat, surrounded by piles of books.

"Hello, Rachel. I've started going through the books. I won't have nearly enough space in my new apartment, but it's hard to think of getting rid of them—they're like old friends."

Rachel glanced at Mark. She'd been right—moving was going to be stressful for Trudy. And they were just beginning.

She spent the next few hours cataloging Clyde's movie memorabilia. His collection included everything from original scripts of some of his greatest films—including penciled director's notes—to a fedora once worn by Humphrey Bogart. The items would be worth a fortune to other collectors, but it saddened her to think of them leaving the family.

While Boris supervised from his position atop the desk, Mark worked with his grandmother, patiently stacking the books in piles after decisions were made. Unfortunately, the *give-away* pile grew at a fraction of the rate of the *keep* pile.

When Trudy fussed he soothed her. "Don't worry, Grandma. I'll find a place for the extras. That way we can rotate them in and out of your apartment whenever you're in the mood. It will be like having your own personal library."

She beamed and patted his hand. "I knew you'd understand. You always have."

Rachel was torn between wanting to hug them both and feeling like an eavesdropper on a touching, private conversation. A few minutes later she stifled a yawn and glanced at her watch. "Wow, the time really slipped away from me. I need to head home."

"Can you come again tomorrow evening?" Trudy asked.

"I'm sorry, I'm afraid I can't. I have to drive my parents to the airport in San Jose. They're flying to St. Louis to see my sister and brother-in-law and their new baby for Christmas."

Trudy frowned. "And you aren't going?"

Rachel shook her head. "I can't take time away from Furry Friends. You know the days before Christmas are the busiest time of year at the shop, and most of the volunteers are too busy to work. I'll go next summer."

Mark stepped forward. "Do you have plans for the holiday?"

Ever since her mom had announced their intentions, Rachel had been trying not to think about it. She'd spent the past five Christmases since her divorce with her parents. She pasted on a cheerful smile. "I thought I'd have a peaceful day at home."

He frowned. "You can't spend Christmas alone. You should spend it here, with us."

"I—"

"You must," Trudy interrupted in a tone that brooked no argument.

Rachel let out a tired laugh. "Okay. I won't try to argue with both of you."

Mark's lips curved in a satisfied smile. "Good. Ten o'clock Christmas morning. It's a date. Come on, I'll walk you to your car."

When they reached the car, he opened the door but blocked her entry. "Thank you for agreeing to join us for Christmas. It made Grandma happy."

Ah, Grandma. Well, she wanted to make Trudy happy.

He bent his head, and his voice dropped to a near whisper. "It made me happy, too."

A tingle ran up Rachel's spine and lodged in her chest. What was going on here? What did he want?

"I'm glad everybody's happy." She flashed a quick smile then slipped under his arm and into the driver's seat. "See you Friday morning."

****

Christmas morning, Rachel once again stood on the front porch of Trudy's house, contemplating the doorbell. This time she was trying to figure out how to push it with a large wrapped package in one hand and a covered food container in the other. She had almost reached the bell with her elbow when the door opened and Mark appeared.

"Here, let me take that." He reached for the domed plastic container.

She straightened, almost knocking it out of his hands. "Thanks, how did you —"

"I was watching from the front window."

He'd been waiting for her. That pesky tingle returned and morphed into a glow.

She followed him into the kitchen, where Trudy stood on a small footstool in front of the stove, frying bacon. Boris sat expectantly at her feet, licking his chops.

"Merry Christmas, dear." Trudy's voice rose above the sizzle from the frying pan and the muffled roar of the exhaust fan. "I hope you like bacon. The doctor says I shouldn't eat it, but what does he know? Besides, Mark loves it."

Rachel grinned. "I love it, too. And I brought homemade cinnamon rolls."

Mark whisked the lid off the plastic container and took a big sniff. "These are huge, and they smell like heaven."

"My father adores them. They're my traditional contribution to Christmas breakfast."

"I'm sure they're wonderful. You can put one on each of those plates." Trudy pointed to three plates already on the serving tray. "I thought we'd eat in the study."

A few minutes later, they sat at the same small table where they'd eaten supper a few days before. Today, a Trudy-sized Christmas tree stood near the elegant plastered fireplace, where a cheery fire crackled.

145

"Mark got the tree and helped me decorate. We had such fun. It was just like old times." A wistful nostalgia filled her voice.

"We'll do it again next year." Mark sounded determined. Rachel hoped Trudy's new apartment would be big enough for a tree.

As they ate, she glanced around the room, checking for progress on the business of sorting and packing. Two boxes of books sat in front of the bookcases, but everything else appeared untouched. The items she'd catalogued had been returned to their places. Her heart sank. Getting ready for the move must be even harder for Trudy than she'd feared. Perhaps she could give her friend something to look forward to.

She set her fork down. "I'll be right back." She hurried into the foyer and returned with the large, flat, wrapped package. She handed it to Trudy. "Here's a little something I made for you. Merry Christmas."

Trudy sent her a quizzical look then ripped it open with characteristic vigor. When the torn wrapping paper fell to the floor, she held up a lovely, framed watercolor.

"It's the view of the ocean from the terrace of Casa de las Olas," Rachel explained. "I painted it for you after our last meeting. I thought you might want a memento to take with you to Cypress Manor."

Trudy turned with tears in her eyes. "It's beautiful, dear. Perfect, in fact. Thank you so much." She angled it to show Mark. He stared at it a long moment then turned to Rachel with misty eyes.

Another minute and we'll all be bawling.

She swallowed hard. "I'm glad you like it."

"I love it. Now I want to share Mark's Christmas present with you."

Rachel hoped it wasn't food. After eggs, bacon, and a giant cinnamon roll, she was stuffed to bursting.

"You tell her," Trudy urged her grandson.

Mark shifted in his chair to face Rachel. "I've decided to buy Casa del las Olas from Grandma."

Rachel smiled in genuine pleasure. It was the perfect solution for Trudy. Mark could certainly afford the place. According to the media, he ranked in the top tier of Silicon Valley tech moguls. More importantly, all the family heirlooms could stay in the house, stay in the family. If he used it as a weekend getaway, she might be able to see him occasionally. The glow in her chest kindled again.

It was such a perfect plan she was surprised Trudy hadn't thought of it. Or had she?

As if she'd read Rachel's mind, Trudy chimed in, "And there's more. Go on, tell her."

Mark cleared his throat. "I'm moving here full time."

Whoa. "Can you run your business from here?" Everyone and his brother seemed to be telecommuting these days, but Mark had an established business with its own building and hundreds of employees.

He rested his elbows on his knees and clasped his hands, absently twisting a gold signet ring on his right hand. "Along with an invitation to his wedding, Leon sent me an offer to buy out my half of El Dorado Technologies. I've decided to take him up on it."

"That's a big step." According to Trudy, the business was his life.

He nodded and glanced down at his hands. "I've put everything into the company for the past fifteen years." After a moment, he raised his head. A new spark glimmered in his eyes. "But I also realize how much it's

147

taken out of me. Work isn't fun anymore—it hasn't been for some time. I realized I don't like running a big business. I like innovating. I like tinkering. I like seeing ideas become reality. And I have some ideas I'm anxious to try without risking employees' livelihoods or investors' money. I can do that from here."

Rachel's smile widened. "It sounds perfect."

He leaned forward and placed one hand on hers. "There's also another big plus."

The glow surged, and heat rose in her cheeks. "Yes?"

"You and I will be able to get to know each other better."

"Yes." Her response came out just above a whisper.

The ring of silver striking glass interrupted the moment, and Trudy raised her half-empty mimosa. "I believe this calls for a toast."

Rachel and Mark grinned at each other as they lifted their glasses.

Trudy touched her glass to theirs. "A very Merry Christmas to us all, and here's to a new year filled with hope and possibilities."

"Hear, hear." Their voices blended in harmony.

"Oh, and by the way, you're welcome. Both of you."

A Hard Luck Christmas

Olivia Castillo gripped the steering wheel, struggling to keep her rusty, trusty old Civic on the right side of the two-lane highway in the gusty, gale force wind — not that there were any other cars to worry about. As far as she could tell, she was the only living soul on this godforsaken road in this godforsaken state.

Western Nebraska had been barren, but eastern Wyoming looked like a scruffy, grass-covered version of the Sahara Desert to a city girl from Chicago. Where were the trees? The only vegetation she'd seen for miles were gargantuan tumbleweeds that danced across the highway and piled up against the barbed wire fence on the southern side. How did people live here? Apparently, they didn't.

Tiny hard crystals of snow flew past her windshield, in too great a hurry to settle on the pale, windswept grass. Even squinting, Olivia could barely see fifty feet ahead. If she'd had any sense, she would have taken the hint when the Highway Patrol closed the interstate and checked into a motel. Instead, she'd turned off on a county road, determined to push on. The sooner she put this wasteland behind her, the sooner she would reach

149

San Francisco. Nothing particular and no one special awaited her there, but the City by the Bay had sounded like a romantic destination when she'd thrown everything she owned into her car and headed west. Every girl needed a goal, especially when life kicked her in the teeth.

A green highway sign appeared in the sea of white. It read: Hard Luck 4 miles. Olivia nearly choked on the irony.

Signs of human habitation began to appear here and there: a gate with a cattle guard, a ranch house in the distance, a country church with a pointed white steeple. And. . .wait a minute. . .was that Santa Claus hitchhiking?

As she drove closer, she leaned forward until her chest pressed against the steering wheel. Up ahead, a tall, rangy man in a Santa suit, complete with hat, stepped into the middle of the road and waved his arms wildly. She didn't see a car, or even a sleigh. How had he ended up out here alone?

Olivia was street-wise enough to know to avoid hitchhikers, even if they were dressed as Santa. A girl didn't reach the advanced age of twenty-nine in the *barrio* by picking up strange men.

But she wasn't in the *barrio*. She wasn't even in Chicago. As far as she could tell, she was beyond the bounds of civilization. The wind was howling, it was snowing, and hers was the only vehicle she'd seen since turning off the interstate. If she didn't stop for him, Santa might freeze to death. She couldn't have that on her conscience.

She slowed to a stop next to the man and leaned over to unlock the passenger door. The Honda's automatic door locks had long since ceased to function. "Get in."

The man slid in and slammed the door, muttering profanities under his breath.

Her chest tightened. It would be just her luck to pick up a dangerous lunatic in the dead center of nowhere. Then she remembered one of her father's favorite sayings, the best defense is a good offense. She scowled and raised her voice. "If you're going to keep that up, you can get out now."

The man pulled off his Santa hat and turned to her with chagrin written across his rugged features. "I'm sorry. I guess I should introduce myself." He yanked off his gloves and extended his right hand. "Walt Hendricks, full-time rancher and part-time mayor of Hard Luck."

Olivia gave his hand a firm shake then returned hers to the wheel. "Olivia Castillo."

He ran his fingers through his thick, dark hair and heaved a sigh. "I generally try to watch my language around ladies. But I swear, as soon as I get my hands on Billy Forrester, I'm going to string him up by his thumbs."

She shot him a sideways glance as she pulled back onto the highway. "I presume he has something to do with why you were hitchhiking in a blizzard."

"He has everything to do with it. He stole my truck. Again."

Her brows flew up. "Don't tell me someone jacked Santa out here in the middle of nowhere."

"I don't know where you're from, but we don't have carjackings around here."

"I'm from Chicago, and we have too many there. Anyway, you said he stole your truck, so I assume you weren't in it."

Walt tried to use his Santa hat to blot the droplets he'd left on the car seat, with little effect. "It was parked in front of the Methodist church about a mile back. Reverend Hauge talked me into playing Santa at the community holiday pageant. While I handed out packages, I noticed Billy in the background, helping his grandma with the refreshments. I should have known." He shook his head. "After everyone left, the reverend and I got to talking about a problem he's having with kids doing doughnuts in the parking lot on Saturday nights, tearing up the gravel surface. Then he got a call and had to leave, and I stepped into the john. When I came out, my truck was gone and my jacket and cell phone with it."

"Why are you sure this Billy person took it?"

"Because he makes a habit of stealing my truck nearly every time I come into Hard Luck for a meeting. I don't know where he takes it, but he always brings it back and leaves it in my parking place in front of City Hall. But this time I wasn't even in town."

"If you're sure it's him, why don't you have him arrested?"

"I probably should, but I can't bring myself to do it. I like the kid and Billy's in a tough situation."

Olivia had known a lot of kids in tough situations. If someone didn't intervene, many never made it out. "He should be held responsible for his actions. He needs to learn about consequences."

Walt stared out the window at the wind-driven snow. "He knows more about consequences than most kids his age. He and his grandmother moved to Hard

Luck from the reservation two years ago to be closer to his mom. She's an inmate in the Wyoming Women's Correctional Institution just outside town."

His words went straight to Olivia's heart, and she sent up a brief prayer of thanks for her own mother, who had recently retired to San Antonio. She'd been lucky— her mom had worked hard and sacrificed every day to give her children the best she could. Olivia's heart went out to any child forced to grow up without a mother's love and care. "That is tough, especially at his age. Children of inmates carry an extra burden."

"You seem to know a lot about it."

She shot a quick glance in his direction and found herself looking straight into sage-green eyes. "I was a social worker for eight years, until last week."

"What happened? Did you get burned out dealing with other people's problems?"

She let out a short, harsh laugh. "No. Actually, I got a taste of them myself. I got laid off. Budget cuts at the county."

"You'd think they could wait until after the holidays."

She shrugged. "That's not the worst of it."

"What's worse than losing your job right before Christmas?"

Should she tell him? The situation was humiliating. Then she shrugged. Why not? It didn't matter what this stranger thought of her. After she dropped him off, she would never see him again. Besides, maybe it would be liberating to say the words out loud. "How about having your fiancé leave you for an exotic dancer—a pregnant exotic dancer."

"His baby?"

She nodded. "Yep."

153

"Ouch."

"Yeah." She peered ahead through the snow that flew across the beams of her headlights. It would be dark soon. She had planned to spend the night in Laramie, but the highway closure and detour had thrown her off schedule. "We must be almost to Hard Luck."

Walt shifted in his seat and straightened. "We are. Do you see those lights up ahead? That's the Texaco station on the edge of town. You can drop me at City Hall. I'm sure my truck's waiting there."

Thunk. Bong. The car shook and the *Check Engine* light glared a menacing yellow from the dashboard.

****

A tiny muscle in the young woman's jaw clenched and released. She squeezed her eyes shut tight, and a hint of moisture glinted under thick, dark lashes. She was beautiful in a slightly exotic way, with smooth honey-toned skin, lush, full lips, and long black hair that spilled over her shoulders in soft waves. But it wasn't her looks that tugged at Walt's heart.

Olivia Castillo had plenty of grit—she'd been brave enough to pick up a stranger on a deserted stretch of highway—yet here she sat, struggling not to cry. He understood. She'd had a rough go recently, and the last thing she needed was car trouble. Everybody had a limit, and she was obviously close to hers.

"It's probably nothing serious." He doubted his words even as he spoke.

She swiped a gloved hand across her lashes. "No such luck. This transmission has been taunting me for the last couple of weeks. I'd hoped to make it to

California and find a new job before it gave up completely."

"Maybe it won't be as bad as you think. If you can coax it along as far as City Hall, I'll pick up my truck and take you to the local garage. If Hank can't fix it, it can't be fixed."

She shot him a skeptical look. "That doesn't make me feel better, you know."

"Trust me. Hank's a genius when it comes to cars. Turn left here."

She pulled into the parking lot of the three-story, tan brick building that housed the county offices as well as the Hard Luck City Hall. As predicted, his truck sat parked in the space marked *Mayor*, innocent as could be.

"That's it. The red one."

"How does he manage to keep stealing it? I assume you don't leave it unlocked."

"Of course not. He must have rigged up some kind of slim jim, then he hot wires it." He opened the door and stepped out. "You can follow me to Hank's Garage. It's only a couple of blocks away."

He drove slowly and kept an eye on the small beige Honda in the rearview mirror. When they reached Hank's empty lot, Olivia pulled in beside him. He climbed down from the cab and knocked on her window. She lowered it with a disgusted frown.

"It's closed," she accused.

The icy wind sucked the warm air from his lungs. The Santa suit and hat offered scant protection. He should have grabbed his jacket from the truck. "Of course it's closed. It's Sunday afternoon. But Hank lives out back. I'll get him. You wait here."

Walt's boots crunched through the hard-packed snow as he hurried around the side of the white concrete block building and pounded on the door of Hank's bungalow. Five minutes later, Hank had opened the garage door, directed them inside, and had his head buried under Olivia's hood.

"What do you see?" She jammed gloved hands into her pockets. Despite the shelter of the garage, each word sent a puff of frosty mist into the air.

"Hmph." Hank straightened then grabbed a wrench, laid down on a slider, and rolled under the front end.

Olivia shifted nervously as various clanks and clunks emanated from under the vehicle. Then Hank rolled out and sat up.

"Do you know what the problem is?" Her voice shook ever so slightly.

"Sure do."

"And…?"

"If I order the part online tonight, I can probably have it by Wednesday or Thursday, depending on the weather. The whole job'll cost you around nine hundred bucks. With luck, we can have you on your way by Friday afternoon." He gave her a cheery grin that revealed a missing tooth on the upper right side.

A stunned look crossed Olivia's face, as if he'd smacked her in the head with his wrench. "Nine hundred? Friday afternoon? But…" She sagged against the driver's side door and covered her eyes with one hand.

When Walt slid an arm around her shoulders, she didn't resist. "Hey, it'll be okay. Let's get what you need out of your car, and I'll take you over to the Wagon Wheel Motel. It's clean and comfortable, and Sally and Bud offer special rates to stranded motorists when the highway is closed."

She glanced up and blinked a couple of times to banish the trace of tears. "I guess I don't have much choice."

"I know this isn't what you planned, but sometimes it's the detours that make life interesting."

Her lips tilted in a wry half-smile. "I've had plenty of those in the past two weeks. What's one more?"

When he saw the glint of humor return to her eyes, a taut cord of tension eased. "That's the spirit. Besides, Sally serves hot, spiced apple cider and homemade gingerbread cookies every afternoon in December, and I know where she keeps a bottle to add a little something extra when the situation calls for it."

Olivia hiked her purse higher on her shoulder. "If being broke, unemployed, stranded in a blizzard in Hark Luck, Wyoming, and staring a nine hundred dollar repair bill in the face doesn't call for a stiff shot, I don't know what does. Let's go."

Twenty minutes later, he had settled Olivia and her gear into a room at the Wagon Wheel, and they sat in the cozy lobby, along with a family of seven from Broken Bow, Nebraska, sipping hot cider and eating cookies. When they finished, Walt pushed to his feet. "I'd better get home before the weather turns worse."

She nodded and rose. "Thanks for helping me."

He took her hand. It was a nice hand — small, but firm and strong — like the woman herself. "You're the one who helped me. Remember? If you hadn't stopped, I might be frozen stiff as a fence post by now." At the sight of her smile, an idea began to form. He gave her hand a little squeeze before letting it go. "There is something more you could help me with, though."

A charming dimple appeared beside her mouth. "I might be able to do that. It appears I don't have much on my calendar the next few days."

He was glad to see her bounce back. There was nothing like Sally's doctored cider and a couple of cookies to improve one's perspective on life. "If you drop by my office at City Hall tomorrow morning around ten, you might be able to lend some professional expertise to a certain ongoing situation."

When he didn't elaborate, she tilted her head and her brows pinched together. "Um, sure."

"Good. I'll see you in the morning. Have a good night." With a firm yank, he settled his Santa hat in place and headed out the door.

****

At nine-fifty-five the next morning, Olivia zipped up her parka, pulled a knit cap on her head, wrapped the matching scarf around her neck, and stepped out the front door of the Wagon Wheel Motel. Yesterday's storm had passed, leaving in its wake brilliant blue skies and a dusting of crystal flakes that sparkled on every surface. In the distance, fresh white snow capped the treeless mountains. For a city girl, the vast openness of the landscape was a bit intimidating, but she had to admit the high plains had a certain stark beauty in the morning sun.

She had no idea what Walt wanted from her, but as she'd said, she had nothing else to do while she waited for Hank to fix her car, and anything beat watching game shows on television in a motel room. Besides, to her surprise, she liked spending time with Walt Hendricks. He reminded her of a Tom Selleck cowboy movie she'd seen on TV years ago. Like Tom, he was tall, handsome, and self-effacing. And the Santa suit had added a nice touch of whimsy. She liked a man who didn't take himself too seriously.

City Hall was only a block and a half from the Wagon Wheel, so she arrived at the reception desk right on time. A round-faced woman wearing jeans and a red flannel shirt ushered her back to the mayor's office where she found Walt sitting behind a sturdy wooden desk. Seated opposite him were a gray-haired man in a police officer's uniform and a slim teenaged boy, teetering on the brink of manhood, with long black hair and a sullen twist to his lips.

As soon as he saw her, Walt rose and escorted her to the only vacant chair. "Olivia, I'd like you to meet Chief Warren of the Hard Luck Police Department, and this is Billy Forrester."

She shook Chief Warren's hand and smiled at Billy, who stared at his feet. When she glanced at Walt, he shrugged, as if to say, "See what we're working with?"

He returned to his chair and clasped his hands in front of him. "Billy, I asked Ms. Castillo to join us today because, as an experienced social worker from Chicago, she's worked with a lot of characters tougher than you. I want her opinion as to what we should do with you."

Billy's head shot up. "What do you mean 'do with me'?"

"Well, having you steal my truck every time you feel like it doesn't work for me. It's inconvenient. And as Chief Warren reminded me, auto theft is a serious crime."

A look of panic filled Billy's dark eyes, and his body tensed as if he were getting ready to bolt. "You got no proof it was me."

"I'm afraid I do. Deputy Clark saw you park my truck in front of this building yesterday afternoon."

Billy gripped the arms of his chair. "But—"

"Just a moment," Olivia interrupted. "I'd like a few minutes with my client in private."

Billy narrowed his eyes. "You aren't my lawyer."

She'd worked with enough troubled teens to brush his bravado aside. "No, I'm not, and if you're willing to work with me you might not need one." She turned her attention to Walt. "What do you say?"

He nodded, pushed back from his desk, and stood. "Come on, Chief. I'll buy you a cup of coffee."

When the men left, closing the office door with a firm click, Olivia turned to Billy. "Tell me what's going on."

His lip curled in practiced adolescent surliness. "I don't know what you're talking about."

"Why do you keep stealing Mayor Hendricks' truck?"

He shrugged and turned his head to stare out the window.

"I assume you'd rather not spend the next couple of years in Juvenile Hall."

"I can handle it."

Billy might be a Native American in a hole-in-the-wall town in eastern Wyoming, but he was essentially no different from the sixteen-year-old Latino gangster wannabes she'd worked with in Chicago. "You might think you can handle it, but can your grandmother? Her daughter's already in jail. Who's going to take care of her if you go away?"

The boy's macho posturing dissolved, and panic returned to his eyes. "They wouldn't really send me to juvie, would they? My grandma needs me. She doesn't get around too good. I have to go to the store for her and get her medicine and stuff."

Olivia had a stirring suspicion. "Why do you take the mayor's truck, Billy?" she asked firmly.

"He's usually a pretty straight guy. I thought he wouldn't mind. . .not too much, anyway."

She shook her head. "That's not a sufficient answer. Why steal any vehicle?"

He dropped his gaze to his feet again. "I needed it."

"To go shopping for your grandmother?"

"Yeah." His voice dropped further. "And to visit my mom."

Her heart tightened. Now she understood. "You time your thefts to visiting hours at the prison."

"When I can."

"So what you really need is a car of your own."

Scorn painted his handsome features. "Sure, but we both know that's never going to happen. I don't have the money and I never will."

Olivia shook her head. Young people could be so absolute in their views of life. What Billy needed was a little re-direction. "Do you like cars—besides just to steal?"

"Yeah." He drew the word out as if he suspected some kind of trick.

"What if I found a way for you to earn some money?"

He shrugged again, but interest sparked in his dark eyes.

"Are you a slacker who would rather lie around playing video games all day, or are you willing to work?"

Billy stiffened and growled, "I'm no slacker."

She smiled. "Good. Then I might be able to do something to help solve your problem."

"What?"

"I'll let you know tomorrow, after I talk to a few people. But first we need to persuade Mayor Hendricks and Chief Warren not to lock you up."

At that moment, the office door opened and the men walked in.

"Have you settled things with your client, Ms. Castillo?" Walt asked.

Olivia rose and pinned Billy with a sharp glance. "I believe I have. I need until tomorrow morning to finalize. If you will release Billy on his own recognizance until then and meet me at Hank's Garage at ten o'clock, I hope to have a solution to everyone's problems."

Walt nodded. "I'm willing. Chief?"

"I suppose we can wait another day, if it's going to make a difference," the chief said.

Olivia flashed them a broad smile. "Thank you, gentlemen." When she turned to Billy, she replaced the smile with a look of stern warning. "And you'd better come, too. Can you get there legally?"

"I'll pick him up," Walt volunteered, slapping an arm around the boy's shoulders.

"Excellent. I'll see you tomorrow."

****

By ten the following morning, Olivia had already had a conversation with Hank at the garage. She checked her watch for the fifth time then resumed pacing, rubbing her hands together and peering out the glass door of the small waiting area. After a couple of minutes, Chief Warren pulled up in a police cruiser. Finally, Walt

Hendricks' red truck drove into the lot. Walt and Billy climbed out, and Chief Warren joined them as they approached the door. When the men stepped inside, the waiting room shrank to the size of a broom closet.

Walt stomped the snow off his boots on the mat by the door. "Here we are, as requested."

Olivia opened the door into the work area of the garage. "I have a proposition, but I think it would be best if we joined Hank before I explain it."

Hank had a gas heater blasting, but it barely took the edge off the chill in the garage. When they walked through the door, he straightened from the car he was working on and wiped his hands on a grease-blackened rag. Four pairs of masculine eyes turned their attention to Olivia, and her stomach did a nervous turn. What if they rejected her plan? She was surprised by how invested she felt in this situation and these people she'd just met.

"Mayor Hendricks, Chief Warren, would you agree it would be better for everyone to give Billy something constructive to do rather than send him to Juvenile Hall, assuming he agrees never to steal a car again?"

Walt looked at the chief, who hesitated then nodded. "Sounds reasonable."

"And Billy, you said you were willing to work."

"Yeah."

"Well, Hank told me he could use some help cleaning up around the garage and handling the cash register a few hours after school during the week and on Saturdays. If you work hard and show promise, he might also be willing to teach you about auto mechanics."

Billy's eyes sparked and he almost smiled. "That sounds good."

She glanced between the three men. "Have we got a deal, then?"

"Sounds like we do." Walt clapped a hand on Billy's shoulder.

Hank stepped forward and thrust out his hand. "You work hard and we'll get along fine."

"Yes, sir."

"One more thing. I got a junker out back that hasn't run in years. If you help me get it going, I might let you take it off my hands."

The boy's dark eyes rounded. "You mean to keep? A car. . .of my own?"

Hank nodded. "Yep. It's not doing anybody any good sitting out there rusting away." He winked at Olivia. "That's what they call in-cen-tive. I expect I'll get my money's worth."

A warm glow blossomed in her chest. She didn't know if Billy would be able to stay out of trouble indefinitely, but he had a better chance now than he'd had yesterday.

"It sounds like we've wrapped things up." Walt glanced at Billy. "Do you want a ride home?"

Billy looked from Walt to Hank and back. "Well. . .it is Christmas break, and Grandma doesn't need anything right away. I thought maybe. . ."

"Why don't we start our new arrangement today," Hank suggested. "You can grab that broom over there in the corner and get busy."

Walt turned his attention to Olivia with a twinkle in his eyes. "I don't think we're needed here. How would you like to join me for a cup of coffee at The Ruby? Ruby makes a killer cherry Danish."

The glow in Olivia's chest flared. "I'd like that very much."

Five minutes later, they were seated across from each other in a booth with red vinyl seats in the most classic diner she'd ever seen. Black and white tiles covered the floor, and the aluminum-banded, Formica tabletop sported a miniature, coin-operated jukebox. A waitress in a vintage-style turquoise uniform with a white apron took their order.

"Cute place." She glanced around.

Walt nodded. "Food's good, too, but that's not the only reason I brought you here."

She raised one brow in a silent question.

"I wanted to talk to you some place less official than City Hall."

Butterflies danced in her stomach. The waitress returned with their coffee and Danish. Olivia doctored her coffee with sugar and cream until it was just the way she liked it—thick and sweet. After the first long sip, she raised her gaze to meet Walt's. "What's on your mind?"

He stirred his coffee. "I know you haven't been in town long and you haven't seen us at our best, but what do you think of Hark Luck, so far?"

Interesting question. She considered for a moment. "I like the people I've met, but there's a whole lot of nothing around here."

A pair of masculine dimples flanked his mouth. "We do pride ourselves on our wide open spaces, but we also have most of the modern conveniences."

"I've always lived in a big city, but as small towns go, this one seems nice enough."

His grin faded into earnestness. "Do you think you could envision yourself living here?"

His question took her by surprise. "I don't know. Why?"

"I like the way you handled the situation with Billy. You care about people, but in a firm, practical way."

"That's what good social workers do."

"Exactly. The thing is, the county's been down two social workers for the past six months. We don't exactly get job applicants knocking down our doors around here."

She drew back and cocked her head. "Are you offering me a job?"

"I would if I could. As it is, I'd like to introduce you to the head of social services for the county. I know she'll be as impressed as I am."

She impressed him. Those silly butterflies picked up their tempo.

"Are you interested?"

Was she? Hard Luck, Wyoming was the polar opposite of Chicago. They probably didn't even have a decent *taqueria*. On the other hand, she'd left looking for a change—a place to start over. Maybe this was that place. "I might be. I would like to follow Billy's case to make sure he lives up to his end of the bargain."

"We can't offer all the benefits of a big city, but you could make a difference here."

All she'd really wanted since graduating from college was the chance to make a difference. What did it matter if she worked in a big city or small rural community?

His smile returned, this time with a coaxing twist. "Is there anything I can say to sweeten the pot?"

"Well. . .I would need someone to show me around and help me find a place to live."

"I'm your man. My family's been ranching here for four generations. Nobody knows Hard Luck better than I do." He held out his hand. "So, do we have a deal?"

She slid her hand into his. "I think we do."

Instead of releasing her hand, he caressed it lightly with one rough thumb. "Hard Luck has a way of growing on people."

Her cheeks warmed, and she smiled. "You know, I can see how that might happen."

Christmas 2.0

Oh, no! Not the dreaded Blue Screen of Death!

Selena Fuller stared at the *Fatal Error* message taunting her from the screen. What had she done? She'd always tried to be a conscientious, if admittedly non-savy, user. She plugged her computer into a surge protector. She tried to remember to blow the dust off the keyboard occasionally. She avoided clicking on funky-looking links. Why would it do this to her now, when she was so close?

She leaned her elbows on the desk in the spare bedroom of her faculty apartment and speared her fingers into her hair. What was she going to do? The final draft of her book was due at the publisher by the first of January. That meant she had less than two weeks to finish and edit the most important publication of her life — the book that would make or break her career, the difference between becoming a tenured professor of Medieval Art at Mid-Hudson College and being unemployed. If she didn't turn in her best possible work on time, she would have wasted the past ten years of her life.

The light from her desk lamp barely extended to the edges of the room. She glanced at her watch. It was a little after seven. She'd been working solidly since lunch. When the writing flowed, time seemed to fade away. But now she'd hit a solid blue wall.

She had long since made peace with her lack of interest in and knowledge of computers, but where could she turn for help? The students and many of the faculty at Mid-Hudson had left last week for winter break, but Selena had stayed to finish her book. She was so close. Just a little more research to do before wrapping up the conclusion. And now this.

She caught her lip between her teeth. There must be someone, somewhere. The little town of Oldebroek, New York, had a few computer service companies, but they wouldn't be open at this hour. During term, techs staffed the College Technical Services office 24/7. But most of the employees were students, so the office was probably closed for the holidays. On the off chance they kept a skeleton crew on call to assist administrators, staff and faculty, she decided to give them a try.

Relief flowed through her body when a live voice answered on the third ring. Selena explained the nature of her emergency, and her knees weakened when the young man told her someone would be over to take a look within the hour. With luck, she would still be able to make her deadline.

As soon as the panic subsided, her stomach grumbled, so she wandered into the kitchen, turning on lights as she went. She loved her on-campus apartment in the century-old, stone building. Besides being charming in an old world, academic sort of way, it was only a short walk to the library and her office in the Art History building. Twelve foot ceilings, leaded glass windows, and dark oak woodwork helped make up for the antique plumbing and heating systems. In the five years she'd worked at the college, she had adjusted to the compact kitchen and tiny bathroom. She would miss the place if she had to leave.

No more thoughts like that. The computer guy will be here soon, and all will be well.

She threw together a quick turkey sandwich, nuked a mug of water for tea, then took both to the small round table in the living room that she used for dining. She was still sipping her tea when a loud knock sounded at the door.

As her hand touched the carved glass knob, she glanced down and hesitated. If she'd been thinking about anything other than the relief that salvation was near, she would have changed out of the oversized Mid-Hudson sweatshirt, penguin-print flannel pants, and puffy blue slippers. In these clothes and with her long blond hair flowing nearly to her waist, she looked more like a freshman than a faculty member. *Oh, well. Too late now.* She could only hope the tech wasn't one of her students.

She opened the door with a friendly, professional smile and found herself staring up into the dark chocolate gaze of…Gabriel Rosetti? The smile fell from her lips as her mouth gaped open. It couldn't be, but it was. She had last seen him ten years ago, almost to the day.

"Gabe." The word escaped and hung in the air like a sigh.

She couldn't take her eyes off his perfectly-carved lips as he spoke.

"Professor."

In college, Selena had loved Gabriel Rosetti with all the passion a romantic, budding art historian could muster. She used to think he was a dead ringer for Michelangelo's famous sculpture of David, but no longer. The boy she'd known had been beautiful, but the man who stood before her stole the breath from her lungs. He still had the same dark curls, heavy-lidded eyes, and seductive lips he'd had at twenty, but now experience had added a confident, grown-up veneer.

"What are you doing here?" she managed.

"You called in the cavalry." He reached inside his black leather jacket, pulled out a business card, and handed it to her.

The card read: *Byte Me Computer Services, Gabriel Rosetti, Owner.*

Of course. Only Gabe would name his computer business Byte Me. She'd bet her favorite cashmere scarf the successful adult was just a façade, and underneath he was still the charming, wise-ass gamer she'd known in college. She raised her gaze to meet his again. "You're the cavalry?"

His lips twitched in a suppressed smile as he nodded.

"That's terrific, but again I have to ask, what are you doing here? I didn't call you. Do you have some super-duper, computer stealth sense that alerts you to systems in distress?"

"Not exactly, although that would be good for business. Actually, I have an on-call contract with Mid-Hudson Tech Services to help out when they're under-staffed or over-burdened. May I come in?"

"Sure." Selena thrust the door aside and stepped back automatically, still struggling to accept the reality of it. *He's here. Now. In my apartment. After all these years.*

"Where's your computer?"

"Uh…oh…it's in here." She brushed past him and led the way to her office.

Gabe shrugged out of his jacket, hung it on the back of the chair, and opened a hard-sided black case bearing the Byte Me logo in red. Selena moved to the side of the desk where she could see his face. He started clicking what appeared to be random keys while staring intently at the screen.

She'd seen that expression a hundred times. He'd worn it whenever he was caught up in the latest video game. Ten years ago it had infuriated her. She'd been convinced he was squandering his time and energy when he should have been concentrating on his studies. Senior year, while she spent every spare minute researching and writing her thesis so she could get into the highest-rated graduate program in her field, Gabe just…played. Exhausted, stressed, and convinced he'd never amount to anything, she'd broken off their relationship the day before the start of Christmas vacation.

Maybe she'd been wrong.

She'd thought of him often over the years—wondered where he was and what he was doing. Wondered if she'd made the biggest mistake of her life by putting her academic career ahead of personal fulfillment. She hadn't had a single serious relationship since breaking up with Gabe. Every other man she'd met had seemed pale and dull in comparison.

His voice interrupted her thoughts. "I think it's a hardware problem."

"What? Oh…the computer. Yes."

His lips twitched again and he lifted one brow. "That's why I'm here, isn't it?"

She nodded.

"Have you installed any new devices or programs lately, or spilled anything on the keyboard?"

"No…um…well, I might have sloshed a little tea, but just a little, and I blotted it right up."

"It was probably enough to do the damage. I've checked my inventory at the shop —"

"You have a shop?"

Annoyance replaced amusement in his expression. "Did you think I ran the business out of my garage, or maybe my mother's basement?"

Ouch. He obviously hadn't forgotten her angry prediction that if he didn't buckle down and work harder, he'd end up living in his mother's basement for the rest of his life.

Heat rose in Selena's cheeks. "Of course not."

"I'll need to pick up a couple of parts before I can fix it."

Another delay. She was never going to finish this book on time. Then what? "How long will it take?" The sharp edge in her voice betrayed her rising anxiety.

He reached for her arm with an expression of concern. "Hey, it's going to be okay. I can stop by tomorrow evening. The repair should take less than an hour."

She sagged against the desk and rubbed a hand across her eyes. "I'm sorry. I'm on a tight deadline, and I have so much to do."

"Do you have something you could work on in the meantime?"

She thought for a moment. "I do need to do one last bit of research. I guess tomorrow would be as good a time as any to go down to The Cloisters."

The Cloisters was a separate branch of New York's famed Metropolitan Museum of Art, devoted entirely to medieval European art and architecture and one of Selena's favorite places. The stone corridors and cloistered gardens always transported her back to the time of knights, ladies, and unicorns. She specialized in the study of fifteenth century tapestries, and The Cloisters had one of the best collections in the world.

"I could give you a lift," Gabe offered. "I get my parts from a distributer in the city."

Four hours alone in a car with Gabe—two down to New York City and two back to Oldebroek. Was she ready for that? She was still wrapping her head around the reality of seeing him again. She lifted her gaze to his and hesitated. Had she just imagined the quick flare of heat in his dark eyes?

"It's no trouble." His beautiful lips curved into a teasing smile. "Come on, it'll be fun."

She'd never been able to resist that smile. She released her breath in a huff. "Well, it would be better than the train, unless you're still driving that rusty, old MG."

He laughed. "No. I caved and bought a real car a few years ago. I'll pick you up around eight-thirty."

****

The next morning, the sky still glowed rosy pink when Selena walked through Mid-Hudson's Gothic-inspired Main Gate to wait for Gabe on the sidewalk. Since the college was built long before the advent of automobiles, parking on campus was always scarce. In the interest of efficiency, they had decided to meet on the main street of Oldebroek, which was also the route to the highway leading to the city. She stomped her booted feet and rubbed her gloved hands together before checking her watch. Eight-thirty-three. He was late.

Selena was always on time — always — but punctuality had never been a priority for Gabe. Even when they were in college his cavalier attitude toward time and appointments had frustrated her. Just as she was winding herself up, a compact SUV pulled to the curb beside her.

The locks clicked, and Gabe leaned over to push the passenger door open. "Hop in."

She climbed in and twisted to settle her backpack-cum-purse in the back seat.

"I'm sorry I'm late." He merged back into traffic.

"You're not — very."

"I know how important being on time is to you, but I got a call from a regular customer and had to assign the job to one of my staff before I left."

"No problem."

Gabriel Rosetti just apologized for being late. On top of that, he has customers. And staff. What is the world coming to?

Pull yourself together. Make conversation like a grown-up. "How long have you been living in Oldebroek?"

"A couple of years. My grandparents live here, and my mom moved back after my dad died."

Her heart contracted. She remembered meeting his father during Parents' Weekend their senior year. He was tall and lean like his son, and his dark eyes glowed with pride every time Gabe spoke. "I'm so sorry. I didn't know."

He shot her a quick look. "There's no reason you would have."

Alison Henderson

She could think of no response, and the silence magnified her regret.

After a few minutes he said, "I didn't know you were at Mid-Hudson until last night. Imagine my surprise when Tech Services gave me your name."

She gave a short, sharp laugh. "At least you had some warning. I almost fainted when I opened the door."

He grinned. "The penguins were cute."

She met that comment with an undignified snort.

His smile faded and he shot her a quick glance. "If I'd known you were in Oldebroek, I would have called."

"I started teaching at the college after grad school. I'm writing a book on medieval Flemish tapestry that I have to finish by January if I want to keep my job."

He nodded. "So your computer situation is a real emergency."

"I'm afraid so."

"No worries. We'll have you back in business by dinnertime."

As they drove down the scenic Taconic Parkway toward New York City, they managed a casual conversation about their current lives, carefully avoiding the emotionally charged topic of their breakup — just two old friends catching up. Selena was amazed by the new, responsible Gabe. It seemed that sometime during the past ten years he'd changed from the passionate, careless boy she'd fallen in love with into the man she'd always hoped he could become. When he pulled up near the museum in Fort Tryon Park at the northern end of Manhattan, she couldn't believe how quickly the ride had passed.

"I'll meet you here at two o'clock," he said.

176

She grabbed her bag and opened the door. "That's perfect." She waved as she watched him drive away, feeling oddly bereft. She shrugged her bag over her shoulder and trudged up the walk to the entrance.

As soon as she crossed the threshold, her mood lightened. Each footstep took her farther back in time and farther away from the worries of the present. The vaulted stone corridors and grand halls banished all thoughts of computers, tenure issues, and troublesome old boyfriends. A mystical tranquility filled the space. She could almost feel her jeans transform into an embroidered gown and her boots into silken slippers as she made her way to the tapestry galleries at the rear of the main floor.

Settling herself on a stone bench in front of a wall-sized tapestry of a fifteenth century hunting scene, she pulled a notebook from her bag. For a moment she wished she had vellum and a quill—her spiral-bound notebook and ballpoint pen seemed jarringly out of place in the medieval setting.

This was her last chance to see the original piece before wrapping up the conclusion of her book, and she wanted to be sure she hadn't missed anything important. As always, the level of detail woven in by the Flemish weavers amazed and delighted her. Every leaf, every flower, every animal had its own special meaning that would have been well known to contemporary viewers.

Selena's pen hovered over the page as she scanned the huge textile, section by section, reviewing each image. Suddenly, a figure in the background caught her eye. She had studied the tapestry so many times—how had she missed the small figure of a dismounted knight? She rose and crossed the room to stand as close as she dared, craning her neck for a better view. The knight appeared to be offering a white flower to a lady, who reached for it while demurely looking away. It had to mean something. There was no such thing as a simple, pretty picture in medieval art. Maybe if she could identify the flower, she could decipher the meaning.

She stepped back, then closer, then back again. The flower looked like a carnation. She would have to check her reference on medieval symbolism when she got home, but if memory served, the white carnation had several possible meanings, including "alas my love," pure love, devotion, and good luck. She pursed her lips. What had the artist meant in this case? If she dug deeper into the life of the nobleman who had commissioned the work, she might be able to answer that question. Her blood hummed in her veins. She loved an academic treasure hunt, and many art historians had made their names from minor mysteries like this. After jotting down a few notes and questions, she headed to the Chief Curator's office for permission to check a couple of sources in the museum's private library.

Several hours later, she closed the heavy tome on medieval French genealogy with a satisfied sigh. She'd found several promising clues and couldn't wait to get back to the Mid-Hudson library to continue her research. Now, if Gabe could just fix her computer… Oh, no. Gabe! She sucked in a quick breath and glanced at her watch. She was late. He might be waiting upstairs already. She scooped her notebook into her backpack, pushed the heavy chair away from the table, and raced toward the broad stone steps. When she reached the main floor, she slowed for a moment to catch her breath and scanned the lobby. *Rats.* There was Gabe, sitting on a wooden bench with an amused expression on his handsome face. He rose to meet her.

She hurried over. "I'm so sorry. Time got away from me. Have you been waiting long?"

He smiled and shrugged. "A few minutes. Then I remembered what happens when you get wrapped up in your work."

Heat rose in her cheeks. He used to say the room could catch fire and she'd never notice when she was deep in her books. In truth, her hair could catch fire and she might not notice.

"I bet you didn't take time to eat, did you?" He reached for her heavy backpack as they walked toward the door.

She shook her head in chagrin. When Gabe draped his free arm around her shoulders as if it were the most natural thing in the world, something familiar fluttered under her ribs.

"I figured that and brought you a pastrami on rye from Manny's," he said.

Memories flooded her. Manny's had been their favorite deli in the Village. His pastrami on rye sandwiches had fueled many an all-nighter.

The afternoon sun warmed the car and drew steam from the highway as they drove north out of the city. Between savory bites of Manny's pastrami, they laughed and talked. Selena shared her excitement at her discovery in the tapestry and her research plans as soon as her computer was up and running. By the time they reached Oldebroek, ten years seemed to have melted away. The sun skimmed the horizon and the air had started to chill again when Gabe parked near her apartment.

"How long will it take to install the new parts?" She stepped up and turned the key in her lock.

"Not long. Then we'll find out if I'm right about the cause of your problem."

She gave him a breezy smile. "I have complete confidence in you." She was surprised to realize she meant it. While she wasn't looking, her sexy, fun-loving college boyfriend had transformed into a full-fledged, competent adult. The problem was he was still sexy as hell. She was shocked to discover that the fire he'd lit in her ten years ago still smoldered, ready to burst in to flames at the slightest provocation.

So what was she going to do about it?

While she pondered that question, Gabe returned his tools to his case then tapped a few keys.

He pushed the chair back from the desk and waved a hand at the computer. "There you go. Good as new."

"Really? It's fixed?" She rushed to peer at the screen.

He raised one brow. "That doesn't sound like 'complete confidence' to me."

"No, no…it's just that…this is so important to me." Relief washed over her as she opened and closed programs and accessed her research. Everything worked. No more dreaded Blue Screen of Death. She grabbed him by the shirt and planted a kiss hard on his mouth. "Thank you."

When she released him abruptly, his dark eyes flared and his lips curved in a smile that melted her insides. "My pleasure."

Selena stepped back and nervously flicked the tip of her tongue over her lips. "Do you want to stay?" She glanced around the apartment. "I can fix us dinner…or something."

His smile deepened. "I've got a couple of things to take care of, but I'll be back later. I've got a surprise for you."

"A surprise?"

He dropped a quick peck on her cheek then walked to the door. "I'll pick you up at eleven. Oh, and bundle up."

At ten-forty-five Selena checked her watch for the umpteenth time. What could Gabe have in mind? Nothing in Oldebroek was open at eleven o'clock at night except the Quickie Mart attached to the gas station on the highway. And why would he tell her to dress warmly? He couldn't be planning to take her ice skating. He'd tried that once at the rink in Rockefeller Center, and she'd spent more time on her behind on the ice than on her feet.

At eleven o'clock she stood by the door, outfitted in down coat, knit hat with matching scarf and mittens, and her warmest boots. The old radiator under the living room window clanged, and she blew a puff of air toward her overheated forehead. If Gabe picked this time to be late, he would find nothing but a pile of winter clothes sitting in a puddle of goo. A sharp knock sounded, and she flung open the door.

His seductive smile did nothing to cool her.

"Hey," he said.

"Hey, yourself."

He carried a small canvas tote in one hand and reached for her with the other to draw her into the hall. "I see you took my advice."

"Yes, and I'm boiling."

"You'll be glad in a few minutes. Come on." He kept a firm grip on her hand as they walked down the hall and stepped outside. The familiar campus grounds had transformed into a magical forest. The full moon glowed like a lighted Christmas ball, bathing the walks, lawns, and trees in silvery light.

181

When they passed the parking lot, her puzzlement grew. "Where are we going?"

"You'll see."

He led her across the quad, past the President's house, and behind the old brick science building to a tall boxwood hedge with an arched opening.

Selena hesitated and peered through the entrance. "The Shakespeare Garden. You've brought me to the Shakespeare Garden."

"I bet you've never been here at night before."

"No." The word escaped in an awed whisper. After the warmth of the day, the evening chill had dusted every surface in the garden with hoarfrost. Every leaf, every twig, every dormant blade of grass sparkled white in the moonlight.

"Come sit down." He tugged her hand and drew her to a stone bench.

Selena was too stunned to resist. What was happening? Had she stepped into some alternate universe? The Gabe she'd known would never have dreamed up, much less pulled off, such a romantic gesture. "I'm speechless."

He grinned and sat beside her. "Good, because I have some things to say, and it can be hard to get a word in edgewise around you."

Her mouth fell open and she started to sputter. "I—"

"Shh." He touched her lips with a forefinger then reached into the tote at his feet. When he straightened, he held a bouquet of white carnations. "These are for you."

Selena took them in silent wonder. Their spiky, white blooms seemed lit from within by the moonlight.

"They stand for pure love," he said. "After you told me about the flowers in the tapestry, I looked it up."

When she still didn't speak, he dropped his gaze to his boots and kicked a pebble on the path.

She reached for his hand and gave it a squeeze. "They're beautiful. Perfect." She blinked away a sudden tear.

Gabe frowned. "Hey, don't cry."

She sniffed—strictly from the cold, of course. "I'm not. But when you said they stood for pure love, it reminded me of our favorite movie in college."

"*The Princess Bride*."

She nodded.

He leaned back against the bench and wrapped an arm around her shoulders. "Is it possible we watched that movie too many times?"

She gave him a watery grin. "Inconceivable!"

Gabe laughed then his expression sobered again. "But Westley never gave Buttercup white carnations."

She kept her tone light. "And that makes you even more romantic than every woman's romantic fantasy."

"I just wanted to show you how I felt, how I still feel." He dropped his arm and turned to face her. "Selena, I've missed you. I didn't realize how much until I saw you again yesterday."

She scanned his face. The moonlight accentuated the strength of his beautifully-carved features. "I've missed you, too."

"When we split up ten years ago, I was hurt, but it wasn't our time. I know that now. We weren't in the same place in life. You were so together. You knew exactly where you were going. I needed time to catch up."

"You seem to have arrived."

He shrugged. "I'm having success doing something I enjoy, but I want more. I'm ready for more."

A shiver ran through her, but not from the cold. "We're in the same place now—figuratively and literally."

"We are." He gently took the flowers from her hand and laid them across her lap. "What I need to know is if you're willing to try again. Are you ready for more?"

Warmth blossomed in her chest as she gazed into his deep, chocolate eyes. He was her first love. Had she ever really stopped loving him? She leaned forward with a smile on her lips and nervous joy in her heart.

Gabe's hands rose to her shoulders, but he hesitated, still serious, waiting for her answer.

"I'm ready," she murmured a moment before his arms tightened around her. His lips met hers in a mix of reunion and anticipation. How could she feel such comfort and excitement all at once?

She vowed this time would be different. Time might have brought changes, but deep down, their love remained. This time they would get it right.

About the Author

I haven't always been a writer, but I have always embraced creativity and relished new experiences. Seeking to expand my horizons beyond Kansas City, I chose a college in upstate New York. By the time I was twenty-one I had traveled the world from Tunisia to Japan. Little did I suspect I was collecting material for future characters and stories along the way.

I began writing when my daughter entered preschool — she's now a full-fledged adult — and became addicted to the challenge of translating the living, breathing images in my mind into words. I write romance because that's what I like to read. The world provides more than enough drama and tragedy. I want to give my readers the happily-ever-after we all crave.

I've been married to my personal hero for more than thirty years. After decades of living in the Midwest, we heeded the siren call of sun and sea and moved to the most breathtakingly beautiful place imaginable - the gorgeous central coast of California. I look forward to bringing you all the new stories this place inspires.

Alison

For details about my other books and news about new releases, I invite you to visit my website at **www.alisonhenderson.com**.

Made in the USA
Charleston, SC
02 December 2016